Die Vicariously
A Voracious Universe Story

Ric Rae

Mind Glow Books

Copyright © 2021 Ric Rae

All rights reserved

The characters and events portrayed in this book are fictitious. Any similarity to real persons, living or dead, is coincidental and not intended by the author.

No part of this book may be reproduced, or stored in a retrieval system, or transmitted in any form or by any means, electronic, mechanical, photocopying, recording, or otherwise, without express written permission of the publisher.

ISBN: 9798450303703

Cover design by: Miblart
Printed in the United States of America

CONTENTS

Title Page
Copyright
Chapter One: Samuel Wheaties — 1
Chapter Two: Jagger Jakowski — 12
Chapter Three: Samuel Wheaties — 21
Chapter Four: Jagger Jakowski — 30
Chapter Five: Samuel Wheaties — 35
Chapter Six: Jagger Jakowski — 43
Chapter Seven: Samuel Wheaties — 52
Chapter Eight: Jagger Jakowski — 57
Chapter Nine: Samuel Wheaties — 70
Chapter Ten: Jagger Jakowski — 77
Chapter Eleven: Samuel Wheaties — 88
Chapter Twelve: Jagger Jakowski — 94
Chapter Thirteen: Samuel Wheaties — 106
Chapter Fourteen: Jagger Jakowski — 115

Chapter Fifteen: Samuel Wheaties	124
Chapter Sixteen: BonnyB-GG	128
Chapter Seventeen: Samuel Wheaties	133
Chapter Eighteen: Jagger Jakowski	138
RESIDUUM OFFERINGS	142
Prologue: Lavesh Dekel	143
Chapter One: Jagger Jakowski	151
Chapter Two: Uma Odia	163
Chapter Three: Jagger Jakowski	172

CHAPTER ONE: SAMUEL WHEATIES

The roto-transport juddered as it descended through the bruised sky of Viribus B to the landing zone. Samuel Wheaties glanced at the other commuters packed in tightly around him. He hated them. He hated how they were happy with their boring lives while he wasn't. He couldn't wait to get home to shrug off his sad life and become someone else.

Samuel exited the creaking vehicle along with the other passengers and think-told Ubiquity to show him the time. 19:05 appeared floating in the space in front of him. His heart sank. *I can't believe I've missed the start.*

The landing zone, or LZ, as everyone called it, was busy. Samuel looked at the hordes of drizzle soaked citizens in his path. Their umbrellas and long jackets were cast in pinks and blues from other roto-vehicles coming into land. Samuel pushed his way through the crowd, his vision downcast, staring at their boots and the occasional flash of neon light caught in a dirty puddle. The LZ was located a block from his apartment, but the mass of citizens blocked his path. Desperately, he shoved his way through the throng, ignoring the looks and calls of protest thrown his way.

Pherson City overflowed with brutal buildings and even more brutal people. People everywhere. If only he could afford to live in a nicer sector. One where the buildings weren't all advertising laden skyscrapers, and the people weren't as numerous. Pherson City was the capital of Viribus B, the only single habitable planet system in the Governance. You'd think it would be nicer.

The entrance to his apartment block was set back from the busy street. Breathing heavily, Samuel stared at the sensor by the door. After a moment, it clicked open. He trod heavily to the bank of elevators and pressed the call button. His rain soaked jacket rose up and down to the rhythm of his breath. Steam shrouded him like a ghost in the empty lobby. He guessed the he'd just missed one. He was thankful he didn't have to cram himself in with other residents. Finally, the old elevator arrived and the rusty metal doors slid open.

"Come on, come on," Samuel muttered, waiting for the doors to shut. He eagerly slapped the button for the hundred and thirtieth floor. Finally, the doors slid shut and the rusty old elevator carried him upward.

Samuel think-told Ubiquity to display the time again. 19:14 appeared floating in his vision via his DigiLenses. He was missing it. This might be Lana Edge's last immersion and he was missing it. He cursed his manager for calling a meeting at the end of his shift. It was bad enough he'd spent all day listening to angry Orinians complain about how their luxury rotocar's auto-bar had spilled a drink. Then to miss the start of Lana Edge's immersion, because the company wanted to brief them on yet another fault in the company's flagship vehicle, it was galling. Samuel shook his head, trying not to think of what he had missed. He scratched the sweaty fold in his neck where his beard rubbed.

The elevator stopped. Samuel squeezed himself through the doors before they were fully open, almost knocking over his neighbor Yuval.

"Watch it, Wheaties," Yuval grunted.

Already halfway down the corridor, Samuel twisted his plump frame back to wave an apology to Yuval when he connected with something.

"Putain!" Geraldina Monette said as she tumbled to the floor. Samuel looked at her. He liked the old lady but didn't have time to help. If he didn't get home soon, he'd miss the whole thing.

"Sorry, Cit Monette," Samuel said, continuing along the hallway to his apartment door.

Behind him he heard Yuval shout, "You knock an old lady over and you don't even stop? There's something wrong with you Wheaties. You're a loser."

Samuel glanced back to see Yuval helping Geraldina to her feet.

"Who you calling old?" Geraldina said, batting Yuval away once he'd helped her back to her feet "Get off me. I can take care of myself."

Samuel closed the door, stepped into his single room studio apartment, and sighed. He checked the time again. It was nearly twenty past. *Damn.*

He shrugged off his wet jacket and let it drop to the floor. Next, he stripped off the rest of his clothes and glimpsed his pale, lumpy, orange-peel like skin in the mirror. His heart sank, and he felt the dark cloud roll over him. Then he remembered what he was doing and pushed away the depressive thoughts bearing down on him. He didn't have time for that. Lana, he was missing Lana. His N-Tac suit lay crumpled on the floor. He picked it up and squeezed his bulky frame into it. The N-Tac suit, or nano-tactile suit, to give it its full name, was one piece of the kit needed to experience immersion. The suit would relay pressure and heat sensations from the immersion experience across the user's body. Another other piece of kit was the immersion pod. Samuel fastened his N-Tac suit up and stepped into the immersion pod that took up most of his tiny apartment. Inside, the pod's fingers connected themselves to the N-Tac suit and lifted Samuel. His immersion pod allowed Samuel to move his limbs, or have them moved in any direction. Last, he needed his uLink node and the DigiLenses. The uLink node that sat on his neck, would connect to Ubiquity and take commands he spoke under his breath, and play sounds via bone conduction. The DigiLenses, which outside the pod overlaid transparent data on top of the world Samuel looked at, inside the pod, the image the DigiLenses displayed was opaque for a complete sense of immersion. Samuel think-told Ubiquity to take him in.

Everything flashed white. Samuel found himself floating in the center of a giant bubble made of thousands of video tiles. It was an awe-inspiring sight, but Samuel didn't have time for that. He'd have to rush if he wanted to catch any of Lana's immersion. He selected Live Immersions, then scrolled the tiles over to the Live Vicariously section. Lana Edge's face smiled out of a tile in his favorites section. He tapped her and cursed at the few seconds it took to bring up her list of immersions. Hurriedly he tapped on the tile at the top of the list; LIVE: My Final Immersion.

Everything flashed white and Samuel found himself standing on a ledge at the top of a skyscraper. The sensations from the sensor suit Lana Edge wore rushed over Samuel's skin. Her DigiLenses captured the incredible view around her for him to see. His heart skipped a beat, and his breathing increased. Nothing matched that first connection into immersion. That rush of your mundane life vanishing as you stepped into the body of a Live Vicariously creator. Especially one like Lana Edge. Samuel felt the immersion pod move his feet, one in front of the other, as Lana walked along the edge of the roof. Lana Edge was one of, if not the best, dare devil sky walkers in Pherson City. He'd been following and supporting her with a hundred credits a month, for over a year now. He couldn't believe this was her final immersion, and that he'd missed some of it. Samuel tried to suppress the rage that was building inside him and instead let the immersion transport him somewhere else. Somewhere with Lana.

Suddenly they were running. The ledge was only thirty centimeters wide, but they ran along it with no fear. Samuel saw the end of the ledge rushing up on them but Lana didn't slow down, instead she sped up and leaped into the air. Samuel felt his stomach lurch as Lana glanced down at the two hundred story drop below them. For a moment, everything was tranquil. Just them, flying through the air together. It was beautiful. Then their outstretched foot connected with the opposite ledge, and they took a few steps to slow down. Samuel felt his groin swell. The adrenalin rush of experiencing Lana Edge sky walk always did that to him. These days, it was one of the few things that did.

Lana turned to face Pherson City. A forest of neon and steel dissected by rows of rotocars, rivers of light in the sky. It was quite a sight. Wind whipped over Lana Edge's body. Samuel felt the tingle of her hair blowing over her sensor suit. This was why he loved Lana. Most guys were into Live Vicariously girls that did porn, but Samuel preferred this. It was more personal, more intimate. Almost as if reading his mind, Lana ran her hand over her thigh and peered at the drop below them. It was electrifying. Then they turned and ran along the roof edge again until they faced another panorama of Pherson City. This time facing north across the richer sectors. The buildings were lower here, and the sky wasn't flooded in neon advertisements. In the distance a gleaming silver band rose behind the city, wide at the base before tapering to a point far, far above. The Hudson/Kiyoshi space elevator.

"It's beautiful, na so?" Lana said. To Samuel her voice was like a waterfall of lush sound, offering him everything in the silence of his immersion pod. Everything he lacked in real life, she gave to him. Non-judgmental connection. A sense of closeness. And of course the thrill of sky walking.

A tap of metal on metal made Lana turn around. There was one security light, but beyond the rooftop was a pool of darkness. It was nothing. They swung back to face the silver ribbon stretching up into the sky.

"Any second now," Lana said, gazing upwards to where the silver reached a point and disappeared. There was a flash of light. Then a twinkling star descended along the silver band, growing larger as it did. As it entered the upper atmosphere, it stopped looking like a star. Now it looked like a pill, growing larger as it traveled down, catching different colors the star Viribus threw along the edge of the breathable film around the planet.

"I'll never tire looking at the Hudson/Kiyoshi

space elevator," Lana said. Then she opened a small bag attached to her hip and pulled out a compact mirror. She held it out at arm's length so she could see her reflection, and her army of fans in the immersion with her, could see her face. *She's beautiful,* Samuel thought. Her teardrop face a rich brown, her large eyes caring and her plump lips always on the verge of a smile.

"I'll never tire of that view, and soon, thanks to you, I'll be going up in one." Now Lana's lips did part in a dazzling smile. "I did it. I got in!"

Samuel felt joy rush through him seeing how happy Lana was, but deep inside, he felt sad. This was it. This was the last time he'd get to live through her.

"I got accepted to New Oxford University on Alexandria. I can't wait to blink to the Orini system and see what it's like. And it's all thanks to you. Your generosity in supporting me for the last year made it possible for me to fund my studies. I'll be eternally grateful. After this immersion I'll leave my fund me account open for anyone who wants to continue helping me, and I'll leave all my old immersions up for you to relive, but this is the last live one. I feel sad. You have all been so amazing to me. I gotta shout out to fans who've made big contributions, or have followed me from the start.

Not in any order, I'd like to thank Lale Avni, Shura Zakharov, Phil Blake, Chui Bamgboshe—"

As Lana Edge continued to list the names of her fans, Samuel felt his chest tightening. He tried to refrain from jealousy, but he hated when she acknowledged other people were experiencing this moment with her, other than himself.

"—Hussien Anwar, Samuel Wheaties, Fujimoto Masaki—"

Samuel's chest swelled and a grin spread across his face at mention of his name. She did care. She was amazing. She really was. Samuel thought he lov—

Lana saw something move behind her in the mirror. They swung around just in time to see red X rush towards them. Samuel felt something slammed into his stomach. Even though the N-Tac suit prevented him from being hurt, the shock of the sensation made him gasp. Suddenly his arms were swinging frantically. For a second, he didn't know what was happening. Then the scream pierced his ears. A terrifying, primal scream. Windows of the skyscraper rushed by as Lana Edge fell, as he fell. Their arms and legs continued to flail wildly. His brain couldn't cope. He tried to curl himself into a ball, but the suit forced him to flap and twist as Lana desperately tried to find a way to stop herself. But she wouldn't be able to stop herself. In the final moments, Lana relaxed and craned her head backwards to look at the silver elevator stretching into space. Everything flashed white. Samuel found himself back in his bubble. He disconnected himself from the immersion pod and stumbled out onto the floor of his apartment. Panting, his body lurched twice, and he died the little death. He tried to stop himself, but it was too late.

What the hell had just happened?

The heat was unbearable. Samuel came to his knees and unfastened the N-Tac suit, peeling it off. He looked down at the mess at his groin. Samuel dropped his head in disgrace. Lana Edge had just died and he... he... he couldn't bring himself to think what he'd done. Shame hung over him. He was a terrible person. Samuel fell to the floor, sobbing. Nothing could bring him back from what he'd just done. Nothing could take back what he'd just spent. He closed his eyes to block it out. But all he saw was the last moments of Lana Edge's life.

CHAPTER TWO: JAGGER JAKOWSKI

"Samuel Wheaties, Fujimoto Masaki, Matthieu Lane—" Lana saw something behind her in the mirror. They swung around. A figure rushed towards them, arms stretched out.

Freeze playback, Jagger think-told Ubiquity. *Rewind in three frame steps.* The dark, hooded figure jerked backwards in time until it came into a pool of brightness cast from a small security light. *Freeze.*

Jagger stared at the figure emerging from the darkness. He or she wore a dark jacket with a hood. The angle of light should have lit the face, but Jagger couldn't see any features. Instead, all that could be seen in the hood was a red X. Jagger think-told Ubiquity to capture the image, then rewind ten frames. The figure traveled backwards, and as they moved into the darkness, the red X faded away.

Interesting, the X only shows when they are in light. Jagger tried to move towards the dark figure, but his body didn't respond. Then he remembered he was in a Live Vicariously immersion. It wasn't a free roaming immersion, where multiple recorders capture a 3D space, to be explored freely. Frustrated, Jagger exited the immersion back to his bubble. He brought up the image of the killer from the immersion. The red X stared out at him. It was expressionless, yet menacing. Jagger sighed. Nothing obvious to identify them stood out.

Jagger exited his immersion bubble and got out of his pod. His apartment was a mess. How long had it been since he'd last picked up? He couldn't remember. Jagger scratched his two-day-old stubble and stretched his other arm out, giving his back a twist. Unfastening his N-Tac suit and peeling it off, he thought about having a shower, but decided against it. Instead, he pulled on some clothes, grabbed his jacket, and headed for the door. A shower, like cleaning up could wait until later. Right now, he needed a drink.

#

"What's zis? Shouldn't you be out solving cases?" Lolo, the owner of Le Petit Zinc, said as Jagger walked into her bar. "It's ze middle of ze day, after all."

Jagger shrugged. Viribus B was an eyeball planet. One side was locked, facing the star Viribus. The star facing side was a scorching desert, while the far side lay a frozen wasteland, and the habitable band around the north-south axis remained in a state of dawn and dusk. For Jagger, without the cadence of day and night, why did it matter what time he drank? Sure, Viribus B had an enforced twenty-four-hour Earth standard day, but most Viribians worked to their own schedule, unless they had a job that required them to follow a 'nine-to-five'. Which Jagger certainly did not.

"I'll take a beer with a side order of mind your own business," Jagger said as he slid onto his favorite stool at the bar.

"Ha," Lolo said. Her maroon colored lips stretching into a smile. "You can mind your own business out of here with talk like zat."

"Okay, okay," Jagger said, holding his hands up in faux surrender. "Just a beer then."

"Zat's better." Lolo moved off down the bar to pour his drink. Jagger threw a look over his shoulder. The bar was in fact empty apart from him, and a couple sat in a circular booth in the corner. He'd been frequenting Le Petit Zinc, in the French sector of Pherson City, since he'd left the military and had come back to Viribus B. And having seen the other two non-sol systems in the Governance, he was glad for the fact that some cultures from Old Earth had persisted here, as they were almost non-existent in the other systems. The Demesnech were forced to forget the cultures of their ancestors on Old Earth, so they could work harder, while the Orinian's only cared about money. Was worshiping money a culture or just a cult? Jagger wasn't sure.

"It's here," Lolo said, placing a golden pint of lager on the bar, snapping him out of his daze.

"Thanks." Jagger picked up the pint and drank a third of it in one gulp.

Lolo watched Jagger with a grin on her face. "So, what makes you so thirsty? Another shit case?"

Jagger shrugged and licked the foam off his upper lip. "Maybe. You hear about the LV girl, Lana Edge, who died last week? Someone pushed her off the roof of the Ziegler Tower."

"Off ze elite condominium? But it's so high."

"Yeah, it wasn't a pretty sight at ground level."

"Oh, mon Dieu," Lolo said, shaking her head. "Ze poor girl. Why would someone do something like zat?"

"That's what her mother wants me to find out," Jagger said, sighing. "She called me this morning. We met in immersion. She said it had been a week and Pherson City Security had done nothing."

"Why doesn't zat surprise me?" Lolo said as she picked up a wet glass from the washer and began to dry it with a cloth. "So, what? She wants you to find ze killer?"

"Yeah. She gave me a copy of Lana—no Grace, Grace Okonkwo, that was her real name. Her mother, Kameke, gave me a copy of Grace's last immersion. She then had to lock it on Lana's LV channel, as people kept reliving the experience."

"Putain. Some people." Lolo put the glass down and leaned on the bar in front of Jagger. "So, you relive it?"

Jagger nodded and took a swig of his beer.

"And?"

"And some creep in a hood with a big X in it, jumps out of the darkness and pushes her. I didn't experience the fall. I… I couldn't."

Lolo nodded. Her lip rose on one side as if she was in thought. "So, are zey doing something?"

"Huh?" Jagger's head was still thinking of Grace falling.

"Security. Do you think zey are actually doing something? Sometimes zey don't want to let on what zey know."

It was a good point. Jagger shook his head.

"You're friendly with Collins, right?" Lolo said.

"Yeah, a bit. But he won't take my call now. He's on shift."

"Well, he normally stomps past here at two o'clock. So," Lolo paused to stare into space. Jagger knew she was checking the time with Ubiquity. "If you leave now and hurry, you might catch him a couple of blocks away."

Jagger smiled. He could kiss Lolo. Instead, he slid off his stool and headed for the door.

"Hey," Lolo called out. "You need to pay for zis."

Jagger pushed the door open. "Put it on my tab."

As the door shut, Jagger could hear Lolo shout, "You don't have a tab!"

#

Cyans, yellows, and hibiscus reds from store signs glided over the chrome body of the security ersatz as it stomped along the street. Jagger had sprinted two blocks from Le Petit Zinc, and now the beer sloshing around in his stomach made him feel nauseous.

"Collins," Jagger shouted. The ersatz didn't turn. Jagger shook his head and sighed. Nausea or no nausea, he had to catch up with the security officer. Jagger put his head down and ran the few hundred meters to the humanoid machine.

Hearing his approach, the ersatz turned and raised an arm. Inside was enough firepower to disintegrate Jagger instantly. Luckily, the weapon never left its housing in the arm.

"Jakowski," Collins' voice said from the head of the ersatz. "You've taken up exercise?"

Jagger couldn't see his face, but he knew Collins, back in the security station where he was controlling the ersatz via an immersion pod, was probably smirking.

"No," Jagger said, bent over with his hands on his knees, trying to catch his breath. He considered patching some Endurance, but didn't want the long effect. Instead, he think-told Ubiquity to give him some CoConfidence. The slim endocrine patch on his arm whirred, and he felt a tiny prick on his arm. A moment later, the drug flushed through his mind, and Jagger stood up. "I wanted to ask you something."

The head of the ersatz was the only part of the machine that wasn't chrome. The shiny black head housed visual recorders and other sensors that scanned every direction. Now it stared down at Jagger.

"Well?"

"Oh." Jagger had expected a protest. "Okay.

Last week a Live Vicariously creator named Grace Okonkwo, though her immersion name was Lana Edge, was pushed from the Ziegler Tower."

The ersatz body straightened slightly. "And?"

"And her mother came to me today saying that security wasn't doing anything about it." Jagger hated talking to these ersatz, you couldn't gage their reactions. "So, are you? Is someone investigating the death?"

"Let me check," Collins said. Jagger was left standing face to face with the metallic security avatar. He guessed Collins was checking their system to see who was on the case, as the ersatz didn't move. He hated these machines. The impersonal nature of them. Which was funny considering how the technology was first developed by the porn immersion industry.

"Yeah," Collins' voice reemerged from the faceless machine. "Looks like Captain Rafi doesn't care too much to waste resources on sex workers."

"Grace wasn't a prostitute," Jagger said. "She didn't sell sex, just her experiences. There's a difference."

"Most of the other officers don't see it that way. And besides, we don't have the personnel to be working cases with low status like this." The ersatz turned back the way it had originally been facing. "Now, if she was an Orinian, then those up high might be more concerned." The security ersatz continued to stomp along the busy street. Citizens cleared a way for the metal beast and threw glances at it as it passed.

"Yeah, yeah," Jagger said under his breath. "Us lowly Viribians don't count for merde."

Jagger think-told Ubiquity to mark the case request from Grace's mother as accepted. If security wouldn't take action to find the killer, he guessed it was up to him. Everyone deserves justice after all, not just the Orinians.

CHAPTER THREE: SAMUEL WHEATIES

Samuel stepped out of Geraldina Monette's apartment into the corridor, just as his neighbor Yuval exited the elevator. Samuel nodded to him and tried a smile, though it felt unnatural. Yuval didn't smile. His forehead creased up in a frown, which seemed to be his permanent expression.

"What are you doing, Wheaties?" Yuval said. Though it was more of a grunt.

Geraldina emerged from her apartment. "None of your business dick sneeze."

"I felt bad about the other day," Samuel said, his eyes locked to the floor in embarrassment. "I asked Cit Monette if there was anything I could do to help her. She said her Ubiquity display wasn't working properly, so I took a look." In the background, they could clearly hear the sound of the Ubiquity display.

Yuval, now stood at his apartment door, one down from Geraldina's, frowned at them. "Isn't that Judge Goode?" Yuval said. "The Live Vicariously pretend Judge?"

"I just watch her," Geraldina snapped. "I don't get into one of those blasted contraptions." Samuel assumed Geraldina Monette was referring to the N-Tac suit and immersion pod. "Besides, it's none of your business, Yuval."

"Actually," Samuel said, trying to break the tension. "I've experienced Judge Goode in immersion. It's good fun switching between the bodies of the litigants and Judge Goode as they argue. Not as much fun as experiencing Lana Ed—" Samuel caught himself from saying her name. "As much fun as a sky walker scaling a building, but still, it's entertaining."

Yuval glowered at Samuel suspiciously. "Didn't one of those LV girls die the other day?"

A lump lodged in Samuel's throat. He dropped his eyes to the floor again and nodded.

"You need to stop liv—" A gaggle of children ran by causing both Yuval and Geraldina to tut and shake their heads. Once they had passed, Yuval brought his gaze back up to Samuel.

"You need to stop living through those virtual girls. You need to go out into the world and actually do something Wheaties." Yuval kept his gaze on Samuel until he was inside his apartment and the door lock clicked. Samuel sighed heavily as he continued to stare at the floor. He turned and made his way to his own apartment at the end of the corridor.

"Don't mind that muckworm," Geraldina

called out after him. "He's just upset because his team lost. I heard him through the wall last night, shouting at his Ubiquity display." Geraldina laughed and closed her door.

As he entered his apartment, Samuel wondered why Yuval thought it was okay to live out his emotional highs and lows through a sports team, but it was not alright for Samuel to do it through LV creators? Hypocrisy. He shook his head and closed the door.

#

Inside, Samuel felt at a loss. Lana Edge used to broadcast a live immersion nearly every day. There were other LV creators he followed but none of them gave him the same feeling of excitement, the same feeling of living that Lana Edge did. He stood in the center of his tiny one-room apartment and gazed around at his pathetic excuse for a life. His bed lay unmade and he couldn't remember the last time he'd washed the sheets. Samuel considered cleaning up, but the thought just made him feel more depressed. No. There was only one thing that would lift his spirits. Lana Edge may be gone, but there were other LV creators out there. He just had to find one he liked.

Samuel stripped off his clothes, squeezed into his N-Tac suit, and stepped into his immersion pod. Everything flashed white, and he found himself back in the comfort of his bubble. He paused for a moment and considered trying out an immersion game. He knew these were highly popular, and by all accounts, someone his age should be playing them. But for whatever reason, they never did it for him. Sure, the experience and storytelling were amazing. But that was just it. A game required you to interact and actively do things. He preferred the Live Vicariously immersions, as you didn't need to think, they did everything for you. Samuel laughed to himself at how lazy that thought sounded, then stopped. It was too close to the truth. Samuel knew he should do something with his life. But the truth was he felt paralyzed by the pressures of living, and the pressure of playing a game seemed just as overwhelming. His dad had called him a loser for not playing immersion games with him. He shook his head. Screw his dad, and screw everyone that didn't understand.

In the Live Vicariously section, Samuel mulled over his saved favorites trying to decide which creator to live through next. They were mostly other sky walkers. But none came close to Lana Edge in shear excitement. Her channel remained active, but the thought of viewing it brought up emotions Samuel couldn't deal with right now. No. He needed something different, something to make him forget about Lana.

A couple of months ago he'd been watching an immersion show that reviewed LV creators, mostly because they had a big feature on Lana Edge, and Samuel remembered the name BonnyB-GG as a highly recommended creator. She was an erotic LV girl. That wasn't normally his preference, but maybe he needed it right now? Samuel think-told Ubiquity to search BonnyB-GG and hundreds of result tiles appeared floating in the bubble in front of him. He selected her channel and looked to see if she was broadcasting live. She wasn't. It didn't matter, recorded immersions felt identical, the only difference was, you didn't have the sense it was happening right now. Samuel ordered BonnyB-GG's recordings by most popular. A Thank You To My Fans, sat at the top of the results. It was from over a year ago, but it had the highest rating. Samuel selected the immersion recording and everything flashed white.

Samuel felt the usual rush of excitement when he entered a LV creator's body. The same tingle across his skin as their sensations flooded his. They were standing in front of a mirror in what Samuel guessed was BonnyB-GG's bedroom. The LV creator stared at herself in the mirror. She had large eyes and brunette hair which cascaded over her shoulders. An intricate neon pink tattoo, almost like lace, ran down the side of her face, onto her neck and down under her dressing gown that was only just keeping her breasts covered.

"Hey y'all, welcome back to my channel," BonnyB-GG said with an exaggerated pout. Samuel laughed in his pod. *Did people find that attractive?*

"I'm Bonny, he's Blithe, he's good, I'm gay. So," BonnyB-GG continued, "Today is going to be a special one. As you can see, my fur baby Blithe's not with me. Yes, It's going to be one of *those* ones. I'm so excited. This one is for my fans only. Because you, my fans, made it possible for me to buy this." BonnyB-GG undid her dressing gown, letting it fall to the floor. It revealed the LV creator's naked, neon pink tattoo covered body. No, Samuel thought, she's not quite naked. You could see a slight sheen on her breasts and other curves.

"It's the Kolff-Ogogic SX34 sensor suit." BonnyB-GG twisted her body while still looking in the mirror so her fans could see her curvaceous behind. "I'm sooo happy. This is going to change things for me in ways I can't even imagine. So, as a massive thank you, I've invited a friend over to help me celebrate." BonnyB-GG turned away from the mirror so they all now stared at her pink satin bed. Another woman lay naked on it. Samuel didn't know where to look. He knew this should turn him on, but he just felt embarrassed. Rather than stare at the woman on the bed, he looked out of BonnyB-GG's peripheral vision to a picture frame on the bedside cabinet. A picture of a dog sat in the frame. A love heart stuck to the frame had the words Bonny loves Blithe written on it. *Weird,* Samuel thought.

A knocking noise made Samuel refocus. BonnyB-GG turned to face the closed door to her bedroom. Then turned to the mirror.

"Oh. Who could that be?" she said with a wink. She turned back to face the door. "Come in." The bedroom door opened and one more naked woman and two naked men walked in.

Exit immersion, Samuel think-told Ubiquity.

Everything flashed white, and Samuel found himself back in his bubble. He shook his head and sighed. This was why he hated erotic LVs. He knew he should feel something, but he didn't. It made him feel impotent. The thing was, he knew he wasn't impotent. It was just…other things did it for him. Like the rush of jumping across a gap two hundred stories high. Or the kick he got out of investigating an abandoned building. It was thrilling. Those were the LVs he preferred. And there was nothing wrong with that, he told himself.

Feeling his heartache, he did the thing he swore he wouldn't do. He navigated to Lana Edge's channel and looked at the list of immersion recordings. They were all there, including her last one, the one where she had died. It was locked. No one could view it. Samuel flicked the recording tiles along, trying to find one that would make him feel something. That would prove he wasn't impotent. He flicked and flicked, but his mind kept thinking about Lana's last immersion. And when he did, his body responded. He hung his head in his pod and sighed. He hated himself, but he had to prove that his body worked.

He exited the Live Vicariously section and think-told Ubiquity to activate his VPN. Once it was running, he manually shifted through some tiles that made up the outer wall of his bubble. It took a while to locate the program, but when he did, he smiled. He tapped it to activate Dark Search.

Technically, accessing the Dark Ubiquity was illegal, but with a VPN to hide your activity, and the right search program, you could find things the Governance didn't want you to view.

Search Lana Edge, My Final Immersion, he think-told Dark Search. The tiles that made up his bubble pulsed through various colors as the program tried to find results. After what felt like an age, but was probably just a few seconds, a series of results came back. Samuel's heart jumped. It was there. Someone had uploaded a copy of Lana's last immersion.

Samuel took a few breaths. Was he sure he wanted to do this? Yes. Yes, was the answer. If this was the action he had to prove he wasn't impotent, then he must do it. He took one last deep breath and went in.

Everything flashed white. He stood in a stairwell, staring at a wall. Then a hand appeared holding a mirror. When Lana's face came into view, Samuel felt himself being torn in two. One part of him felt elation at seeing her beautiful face again, the other part felt despair at knowing the events about to unfold.

"Welcome back, everyone," Lana said, her face blossoming into a heartbreaking smile. "Today is a special day. And because of that, I wanted to do something special for you. I know I always said my dream was to sky walk the Ziegler Tower, but every time I tried I got kicked out by building security.

Well, watch this." Lana put the mirror away and pushed open a fire exit. She stepped out into the darkness, then turned to show her fans the view out over Pherson City. She ran and leaped up onto the ledge that ran along the edge of the building.

Samuel felt a thrill rush through his body, including a certain tingle in his groin. Lana Edge stared out over the city and started talking about her last year as a Live Vicariously creator. Samuel should have been interested. He'd missed this part of the immersion on his initial viewing, but knowing what happens in just a few minutes completely distracted him. He hated it, but his mind kept on thinking about the feeling he'd felt when he fell out of his immersion pod. The ecstasy, that at the time, he couldn't admit he'd felt.

With only the slightest acknowledgment of the regret he might feel later, Samuel think-told Ubiquity to jump to the final twenty seconds of the immersion recoding.

Suddenly he was standing on a ledge, looking out at the Hudson/Kiyoshi elevator stretching up into space.

"It's beautiful, isn't it?" Lana said, and Samuel immediately felt his body respond. He was panting now. The anticipation of what was about to happen was almost too much. But he held himself. The moment she fell would come soon enough. Just like him.

CHAPTER FOUR: JAGGER JAKOWSKI

Jagger floated in the center of his bubble, watching a video tile, which hovered in the space in front of him.

"—and in a dramatic game this evening Pherson City beat Glencore, seven six, in what looks like Glencore's managers last game for the team. Tap now to enter immersion and relive the game in full."

Jagger reached out to tap the blinking button floating in front of him, but stopped at the last second. He had too many cases on and wasn't making enough progress. For the last two days, he'd been trying in vain to locate the studio that was broadcasting the pleasure immersion that Felice Duchamps' father said someone had forced her to do. Security wasn't doing anything about it, as the pleasure immersion had a digital signature from Felice Duchamps stating she had chosen to be there. Her father says they had forced her to sign it, and she was being forced to perform acts she would never do of her own accord. Jagger knew that some pleasure immersions would kidnap girls and force them to perform. And if security weren't doing anything about it, he'd have to find the location of the immersion studio and free Felice Duchamps himself.

"—and in other news," the news anchor continued. "A second Live Vicariously creator, Delilah Dare, has been found dead, just a week after someone pushed Lana Edge off a building. Security have locked Delilah Dare's immersion, though her fans say she was about to climb down from the top of the Hudson/Kiyoshi space elevator when a hooded man with an X mask on attacked her. He used a security binding to attach her to the roof, where they then left her. When the elevator rose upwards to space, Delilah Dare rose with it. The entire sequence was experienced by her immersion users as she was still broadcasting. Live participants say the broadcast kept running for some time after Delilah Dare had passed out, though it eventually stopped working." The newscast showed the grounded Hudson/Kiyoshi space elevator with a white tent covering the crime scene.

"Captain Rafi of Pherson City Security spoke earlier." The image cut to a conference room with the security captain standing on a podium in front of the Pherson City Security emblem.

"If anyone has information regarding the hooded man, we urge them to come forward. But rest assured, we will catch this cowardly killer.

Pherson City Security is the best in all the Governance." Captain Rafi's stern face stared out of the video tile before the scene changed to that of a smiling woman.

"Now to our feature section with Judge Goode. Is the term residuum offensive? Campaigners from the Demesne system say yes, while thinkers from the Orini system say it is an accurate term to describe the fore-bearers of the Demesnech and it is not meant to be derogatory. In fact—"

Jagger think-told Ubiquity to stop the newscast. The video tile rushed away from him and joined the others that formed the bubble of tiles surrounding him.

Another LV girl had died. Jagger shook his head. That couldn't be a coincidence. He'd been so distracted with the pleasure immersion case that he hadn't spent much time searching for Lana/Grace's killer. A girl was being pleasure trafficked and now another killing. No doubt there would be more. He hated having to choose between cases, both intriguing in their own way. He knew security said they were investigating, but he had a feeling they wouldn't take it seriously. Especially if they were spouting that spiel about being the best security in all the Governance. What a joke.

No. Jagger decided he'd have to come back to Felice Duchamps' case. There was a killer out there, and it was anyones guess when they would kill again.

#

Jagger wished he hadn't answered the call on his Ubiquity display on his wall. Kameke Okonkwo's angry face appeared in front of him, her forehead creased under the colorful headdress she wore.

"—and another girl dead. I'm telling you, over a week ago there is a killer out there. And what you be doing?"

Kameke Okonkwo had been ranting for a full minute, so when she stopped, it was a shock to Jagger.

"Um, uh, I..."

Kameke Okonkwo waved her hands. "I see. Grace no mean nothing to you."

"No, no Cit Okonkwo," Jagger said. "Grace's death is important. I've just been very busy."

"So busy, huh," Kameke Okonkwo pushed her lips forward in a look of disgust. "So busy, that more girl done die."

"I'm sorry Cit Okonkwo." A sad look fell over Jagger's face. "I don't know what else to say."

"Abeg you, Cit Jakowski. Death is a robe that everyone has to wear, but Grace had it forced on her too soon. I'm asking you. Please find Grace killer, before more people die." Kameke Okonkwo cut the call, leaving Jagger alone at his table staring at the Ubiquity recorder on the wall. She was right. Pherson City Security didn't seem to care there was a murderer on the loose. So, it fell to him to do something.

CHAPTER FIVE: SAMUEL WHEATIES

Geraldina Monette smacked Yuval with her walking stick as her neighbor retreated from her door. Samuel, who'd just exited the elevator and was making his way along the corridor, squeezed himself to the side to allow Yuval to pass.

"What's going on?" Samuel said as he got to Cit Monette's door. But it wasn't Geraldina Monette who answered. Instead, Yuval swung back to face them.

"What's going on is that Cit Monette is an ungrateful old hag. That's the last time I bring you your packages." Yuval shook his head, then slammed his door, nearly breaking the flimsy metal.

"Why don't you like him?" Samuel said to Geraldina. "He's always nice to you."

"I don't trust him," Geraldina grunted. "I know his sort."

Samuel wondered what she meant by that, when the old woman gripped Samuel's jacket and with surprising strength, pulled him a half meter into her apartment.

"That's why I always keep one of these by the door."

Samuel looked down. Geraldina had pulled the drawer of an old-fashioned sideboard open, revealing a gun. A stiffness fell over Samuel's body. He'd never seen a gun before. The Governance didn't permit private citizens to own them. He couldn't imagine how Cit Monette had managed to procure one. Shocked, Samuel stumbled back into the corridor. As he did, a notification appeared in his vision. It was an immersion request from someone calling themselves Jagger Jakowski. Samuel half laughed at the name. Then he read the reason for the request. Jakowski said he was investigating Lana Edge's death and wanted to speak to her fans. Samuel's first instinct was to reject the request. He didn't know who this Jakowski was, and didn't feel like talking to anyone, especially not concerning Lana Edge. Then he wondered if rejecting the request would make him look suspicious. He certainly didn't want anyone investigating him.

"Sorry, Cit Monette," Samuel said, stumbling down the corridor. "I have to go. I have a call coming in."

"Okay, Samuel," Geraldina smiled at him as he retreated. "You be good now."

#

Everything flashed white. Samuel found himself standing on a wooden floor stretching as far as he could see. Above him a generic blue sky with the occasional cloud met the wooden floor at the fake horizon. This was cheap. The incongruent choice of textures made Samuel think Jakowski didn't care about impressing his visitors. He turned around. A desk and two chairs sat alone in the vast space. A man leaned against the desk. He had pale skin and dirty blue eyes that were sunk under what Samuel guessed was a permanently creased brow. Swept back brown hair and a beard, along with the eyes, gave the man an intense look.

The man pushed off the digital desk and held a hand out to Samuel.

"Cit Wheaties, Jagger Jakowski, Immersion Investigator. Thanks for accepting the meeting request."

Samuel took Jakowski's hand in his and tried to give a firm handshake, but he missed timed it and Jakowski ended up squeezing his fingers.

"It's okay. Call me Samuel," Samuel said, pulling his hand away in embarrassment.

Jagger motioned to a chair on one side of the desk as he took the other. Samuel sat as instructed. The chair was too small for his large frame, making it uncomfortable, but of course not painful. He wondered if this immersion allowed him to alter the size of the chair, but then decided against trying. He already felt embarrassed without bringing attention to the fact the chair was inadequate for him. Then the thought crossed his mind that Jakowski had purposely constructed a chair too small. An intimidation tactic. He shook his head to get rid of the thought.

"So," Jakowski said, leaning back in his chair. "As I said in the meeting request, I'm investigating Lana Edge's death. How long had you been a fan of hers?"

Samuel opened his mouth to answer, then stopped. Something wasn't right. "How do you know I am a fan of Lana's? Isn't that information private?"

Jagger Jakowski let his chair drop forward, making a hard sound on the wooden floor. "Kameke Okonkwo, Grace's mother, hired me. She gave me access to her account," Jakowski said. "Besides, Grace acknowledged you by name in her last immersion."

"Who's Grace?"

A smile crept up the side of Jakowski's face. "Grace Okonkwo was Lana Edge's real name. Kameke doesn't think Pherson City Security are doing enough to catch her daughter's killer. So," Jakowski said leaning back in his chair again, "how long have you been a fan?"

Samuel let the information wash over him. Grace. It had never occurred to him that Lana Edge wasn't her real name, but now he thought about it, of course none of the Live Vicariously creators use there real names. He suddenly felt foolish.

"I... I found Lana, Grace, about a year ago. I had always preferred the Live Vicariously creators to any of the immersion games. There's something about stepping into the skin of another person, about seeing how they lived their lives that was so... personal. Like, I feel like I know these people. They're like friends, you know?"

Jakowski stared at Samuel. A small smile raised his lips, and he nodded.

"Initially, I didn't like the idea of following a sky walker," Samuel said, shaking his head. "I'd never liked heights. But one of Lana's immersions appeared in my feed, and I thought, why not? So, I went in. I'll never forget the sensation of being in Lana's body as she climbed out of a window, and walked along the edge of a building. It was only ten, maybe fifteen stories high, nothing compared to what she'd end up doing, but it was enough. My heart was beating so hard in my chest that I thought I'd have a heart attack. And the great thing was, that's how Lana felt too. She was new at this, and her fear and excitement were so genuine, so honest, that it made living her experiences unique. Electrifying." Samuel stared at the blue sky and realized he had a huge smile on his face. Embarrassed at his rambling, Samuel brought his gaze down to his knees and dropped the smile. "So, about a year. I'd been her fan for about a year."

"Okay," Jakowski said in a voice loud enough to make Samuel raise his gaze. "Her death must have been quite a shock. How did it make you feel?"

The air stood still as Samuel felt his chest tighten. Did Jakowski know he'd been getting himself off, reliving the experience of Lana's death? No. The investigator couldn't know that. He was just asking questions.

Samuel looked up at Jakowski. "It was the worst thing I've ever experienced. I lov—I really liked Lana. She was like a friend to me. To not only know she died, but to experience her death with her, it was heartbreaking."

"I understand." The immersion investigator nodded. "Is there anything you can think of that could lead to the killer? Any fans that were angry with Lana? Any other LV creators she had a grudge with? Anything else that could help identify who did this to her?"

Samuel thought about telling Jakowski that someone had put Lana's death immersion up on the dark Ubiquity, but decided against it. It might get removed, and what difference would it make?

"No. Everyone loved Lana. She was respected in the LV community. I can't see another creator doing this. But I guess you never know. Look, I should get goi—"

"I see. It's just after Delilah Dare's death, any information might help."

Samuel's mouth opened and his eyes widened.

"Oh," Jakowski said, leaning forward. "You didn't know?"

"I don't watch the newscasts," Samuel said, shaking his head. "How?"

"Someone jumped Delilah when she was sky walking on top of the Hudson/Kiyoshi space elevator. He tied her to the roof and let the elevator rise with her still on top."

Samuel suddenly became aware of his N-Tac suit gripping his skin in his immersion pod. He needed to wrap this up. He needed to see if anyone had uploaded Delilah Dare's death to the dark Ubiquity. He needed to make himself feel again.

#

Back in his bubble, Samuel switched on his VPN and brought up the Dark Search program. He'd told Jakowski someone had put Lana Edge's last immersion on the dark Ubiquity. If there was a killer out there, maybe that would help catch them. But now he only had one thing on his mind.

Samuel pushed aside thoughts of morality. She was already dead after all, and think-told Dark Search to find Delilah Dare's death immersion. She might be dead, but Samuel had found something that made him feel alive. Sexual gratification had never interested him, but now he'd discovered how it made him feel, how that moment of the little death brought an ecstasy juddering across his body unlike anything he had felt before, how could he not experience it again?

The results floated in front of him. Samuel think-told Ubiquity to disable immersion control of his right arm. He wanted to be able to pleasure himself while he experienced Delilah Dare's last moments. Samuel tapped the result tile and everything flashed white.

CHAPTER SIX: JAGGER JAKOWSKI

The sound of Delilah Dare struggling was heart breaking. As the Hudson/Kiyoshi space elevator juddered, then started to move, Delilah's fight against the binding became more frantic. Pherson City dropped away, and the sky rushed towards them. Jagger paused the immersion playback. He'd experienced the part where the killer had bound Delilah. He didn't need to live through her death.

Samuel had been right about someone uploading a copy of Lana Edge's final immersion to the dark Ubiquity. After he'd found it, Jagger searched for Delilah Dare's last immersion. He looked to see who had uploaded them. Maybe it was the killer, he thought, but the immersions were transferred to the dark Ubiquity anonymously. The decentralized file sharing dark Ubiquity network meant it would be nearly impossible to track it's origin.

Jagger decided to focus his attention on finding clues about the killer. He took image captures from Delilah's immersion, looking for anything that would give him, or her, away. So far, nothing stood out. Flicking through the images while floating in his bubble, Jagger think-told Ubiquity to identify the clothing the killer wore. After a few seconds, results appeared in front of him. Ubiquity had identified the jacket, trousers and boots. Unfortunately, there was nothing unique about them. Each item was produced by a very common brand and could be purchased in any K-Emporium clothes outlet. Unless the killer was wearing the red X mask while purchasing them, the clothes were a dead end.

What is the red X about anyway, Jagger thought? He think-told Ubiquity to zoom in and enhance the image. The X appeared to be made of a reflective material cut and sewn by hand into a mask. Reflective materials were fairly common. They were used by all sorts of maintenance contractors and construction workers. *So, maybe the killer worked in construction? Great,* Jagger thought sarcastically. *That narrows it down to only a few thousand people.*

He stretched out his arms and legs in his bubble and heard them crack. When was the last time he'd done any exercise? He considered entering a fitness immersion, but the thought of doing calisthenics or strength training really didn't appeal to him. Instead, he exited his immersion bubble and climbed out of his pod. One thing about the killer that had confused Jagger was their lack of Ubiquity activity. Everyone one was connected to Ubiquity. You needed to be, to do anything in the city. But at both Lana's and Delilah's deaths, there had been no Ubiquity activity apart from theirs. Even criminals wore a uLink node, they just normally used a fake profile or had some sort of masking that would make it hard to identify them. But killer X was completely silent, which meant they either didn't wear a uLink node, or they had military grade cloaking.

Jagger peeled off his N-Tac suit. He knew a guy in Sector 4 who sold fake profiles. He'd go see him and ask about anyone purchasing military grade cloaking. But first he needed a shower. He'd been in his N-Tac suit for too long and was smelling quite ripe.

#

The SkyTaxi juddered in the winds that cut through Pherson City's perpetual sunset sky. Jagger stared out of the automated taxi's dirty window at the lanes of rotocars flying around the buildings. There were lanes for auto-controlled rotocars and lanes for manually piloted ones. The manually piloted rotocars were certainly more erratic than the ones controlled by the vehicle AIs, but they were more fun to drive. Not that many citizens could afford to own a rotocar, not on Viribus B anyway. The Orini system might be different, but here most citizens traveled by SkyTaxis or roto-transports.

The automated SkyTaxi was fine with Jagger. It gave him time to think. Why was the killer attacking LV girls? Usually serial killers picked victims that attract little attention. It's easier to keep on killing if no one can connect the killings, or if they don't discover them at all. This was the opposite. Killing LV girls while their fans were living their experience wasn't being careful. It was as if the killer wanted people to know it was him. But if he was the type of killer who wanted to show off, to taunt security, then why hadn't he contacted them?

Jagger picked at the pealing faux leather that

covered the SkyTaxi's backseat. He knew that young people who killed animals, or were into voyeurism, had a high likelihood of becoming serial killers. The voyeurism was part of a need to have control over another human being. To watch people without their knowledge gave them a sense of dominance. Jagger figured experiencing the Live Vicariously girls was a form of voyeurism. But why take it further and kill them? Was it to fully dominate them? Jagger didn't know, but he made a note in Ubiquity to check the backgrounds of Lana Edge's fans, to see if security had arrested any for voyeurism in their past.

The sensation of Jagger's stomach rising made him grip the seat of the SkyTaxi, as it descended out of its lane down towards an LZ. After landing with an unceremonious thud, Jagger stepped out of the SkyTaxi, placing his boot in a neon colored puddle on the tarmac. The landing zone bustled with life. Packs of youths rolled along, laughing and shouting. Street sellers hawked their goods. Scantily clad dancers, a spillover from the erotic immersion studios Sector 4 was famous for, gyrated in window fronts. And the smell of cuisines from the four habitable systems, wafted through the air. Jagger flicked his collar up. He didn't want to draw anyone's attention, then made his way through the energetic crowd to the Jia Mo Noodle Bar.

A cyan neon strip lit the counter that acted as the bar's storefront. It was busy. Jagger hadn't thought to check the time before he left, now regretted it. The noodle bar was three deep, with people jostling to get their order in. Steam swirled and the occasional spit of fire erupted from the kitchen only a meter from the counter where the patrons sat.

Jagger pushed through the crowd, making sure only to annoy youths he thought wouldn't react, or if they did, would be put off by his hard, I don't give a merde, stare. He squeezed himself to the counter, under an orange lantern that hung just inside the bar, and waved at the small woman taking orders. She was of Laos decent from Old Earth, he believed, but wasn't a hundred percent sure. Either way, she ignored him and continued to take orders from customers who hadn't pushed in.

After several minutes, the small woman finally approached Jagger. Her eyes, which he was sure were beautiful when she wasn't working, gazed at him with impatience.

"Khuaam lab tam maak hoong," Jagger said over the din of the street noise.

The woman's already thin eyes narrowed further.

"We don't do that here," the woman said before moving on to another customer. Jagger reached out over the counter and caught the woman's shoulder. She swung around and reached for a meat cleaver that lay just inside the bar. Jagger released his grip and put both hands up to show he meant no harm.

"I've had khuaam lab tam maak hoong here before," Jagger said, trying not to look at the cleaver. "Tell chef Xiong it's for Jagger Jakowski."

The woman held Jagger's gaze for a second, before disappearing into the swirling steam of the kitchen. Next to Jagger, a large unshaven man rotated his enormous head and frowned his scar marked forehead at him.

Jagger shrugged. "I really like that dish."

Before the brute could speak, the small woman

reappeared.

"Your order will be ready over there," she said, gesturing to a door adjacent to the bar. Jagger nodded thanks, but the woman had already moved on taking orders. Jagger squeezed out of the crowd and made his way to the door that led to Phet Xiong.

#

Phet Xiong's face was lit by the pink glow of a Ubiquity display in an otherwise dark workshop. His jaw bulged as he chewed on a stimulant leaf. Jagger never understood why some people did that when you could just administer some CoConfidence or BeAlert via the endocrine patch. Xiong could certainly afford one.

A clang of metal rang out as Jagger's foot collided with something on the floor. Xiong finally looked up from his display towards Jagger.

"You mind not destroying the place?"

Jagger dropped himself into a chair in front of Xiong's desk. "You keep this place tidier and I'll try not to."

A smile broke out on Xiong's face. "It's good to see you, Jagger. You need some more profiles?"

Jagger preferred to do his immersion investigation work using his own profile. That way if he needed to present information to security it was all legit, but occasionally the work required him to go places, or visit immersions, that he'd rather not be id'd in.

"Not today, Xiong. I need to know if anyone has bought military grade cloaking from you recently?"

The smile dropped from Phet Xiong's face. He

turned his head and spat his used up stimulant leaf into a bowl on the floor. When he reached forward to resupply from a tin on his desk, Jagger saw the man's fist was now bionic. The membrane covering it was translucent with a faint hexagon pattern. Inside, the mechanical workings and wires were visible. Jagger heard Xiong had got in trouble with Loup Sokolo, a local crime boss that some believed had connections to the Governance. Either way, it appeared Xiong had pissed him off enough to lose a hand.

"That's why you're here? To ask me questions?" Xiong said. His bionic hand pinched some leaf in the tin and placed it into his mouth. "I sell stuff. I'm not an education immersion."

Jagger laughed and shook his head. He reached forward and picked up the payment code block that lay on Xiong's desk. "This your latest one?"

Xiong nodded. Jagger stared at the abstract payment code on the plastic block and his Digi-Lenses immediately recognized it. In Jagger's vision, text appeared floating next to the abstract code, asking if he would like to make a payment. Jagger agreed he would and think-told amount. Once the confirmation came back, he returned the plastic code block to the desk.

"Okay," Jagger said, gazing into Xiong's eyes. "Here's one thousand credits."

Xiong held Jagger's gaze and smiled. "No. I don't sell military grade cloaking. I don't want to get busted by security. I just sell fake profiles. You know, so you can visit all those less than legal immersions without it being permanently on your record. Why? Who's been using cloaking?"

Jagger shook his head. That must have been the easiest anyone had fleeced him for a thousand credits.

"I don't know if they have used cloaking or just not worn a Ubiquity connection. It's the person who killed the two LV girls."

"Oh yeah," Xiong said, turning back to the glow of his Ubiquity display. "I'd heard about that. Sometimes the simplest answer is the right one."

The muscles in Jagger's jaw tensed as he clenched his teeth, trying to hold back his annoyance at Xiong. He went to stand when he thought of something else.

"You don't know anything about unscrambling point of origin of immersions on the dark Ubiquity, do you?"

"How come?" Xiong said, his eyes not leaving his display.

"Someone has been uploading the LV girl's last immersions, the ones where they die, up to the dark Ubiquity for everyone to relive. I wonder if it's the killer?"

"Jesus, no," Xiong said, turning towards Jagger. "The whole point of the dark Ubiquity network is that it scrambles the location. There's no way to unscramble it."

"Okay, thanks for nothing." Jagger stood and walked back the way he came. His foot smacked into the same metal object as he had when he entered.

"Hold up."

Jagger stopped and turned back to face Xiong's pink lit face.

"It may scramble the location, but if this guy is an amateur, he may have left the original metadata in the immersion code. It might give you the UP address of the recorder used to produce the immersion."

Jagger sighed. "The Live Vicariously girls were the recorders."

"But if the killer copied and uploaded it to the dark Ubiquity, it might have picked up some extra meta-data along the way?"

Jagger scratched his stubble, then nodded. "Thank Xiong. That's worth checking out."

Xiong turned back to his display. "I hope that was worth your thousand credits? Now try not to smash anything else on your way out."

CHAPTER SEVEN: SAMUEL WHEATIES

With the shower set to cold, Samuel aimed the jet of water to his crotch. It stung initially, but the cool water then helped to numb the soreness. Feeling some relief, Samuel stepped forward and let the water rain down on the crown of his head. He knew he shouldn't do it, but he couldn't help it. The feeling of climaxing as Lana or Delilah died was unmatched by any sensation he'd felt before. Perversely, it made him feel alive. In the moments after, remorse would try to creep in, but he forbid it. He wasn't doing anything wrong. He hadn't killed those girls. In fact, their deaths were bringing him comfort. More than that. They were giving him a new energy he'd never felt before. So, in a way, he was honoring them. Of course it was terrible they had been killed, but that had happened already. It wasn't his fault. And his act of using them was keeping their memory alive and giving him hope.

#

Samuel lay on his bed, watching a newscast his DigiLenses displayed a meter from his face. He'd grown tired of sitting in his N-Tac suit in the immersion pod. Now he lay naked, his vast mass taking up most of his single bed, scanning through newscasts trying to find reports on any new killings.

"Is it time the Governance did something about Hari Bhat?" the female news anchor said. Her hair, piled up on her head, created a tall structure Samuel thought looked ridiculous, but seemed in fashion for the wealthier Orinians. She was talking to a political commentator about a Demesne factory worker who'd been badly injured in a chemical accident in his youth and now stirred up trouble with a series of immersion speeches critical of the Governance. Samuel think-told Ubiquity to switch to the next newscast.

It wasn't that he was bored of reliving Lana or Delilah's deaths, but he realized now he'd over used them. That exhilarating feeling that rushed across his body wasn't the same any longer. So he watched for a fresh killing. This time he wouldn't waste it. He'd ration out his use of it, so not to dull the sensation too quickly. Of course, he wasn't willing anyone to be killed. That would be wrong. But if one did occur...

Samuel picked up a pani puri that sat in a takeout carton next to him and popped it in his mouth. As he crunched down on the delicious street snack crumbs from the crispy shell fell onto his chest.

"—and tell me. How scary was it, being inside Lulu Love's LV immersion when this happened to her?"

Crumbs from the pani puri that weren't captured by his rolls of flesh, fell onto his bed as Samuel hurriedly sat up. His heart jumped in his chest. *It's happened again!*

The newscast cut from the male news anchor to a pale-looking man in his forties.

"It was scary, I tell ya," the man said, scratching the beard on his neck. "Lulu, she weren't doing nutin' wrong. We were walking over to her friend's house to do a, uh... performance for us. She's always good like that. Builds it up slow like, so you feel the excitement when she gets to where she's going and uh... uh... the performance starts."

"Okay," the news anchor said, clearly eager to get to the action. "But can you tell us what happened with security?"

Security?

"Uh... Oh yeah, so Lulu is down walking along the riverbank, when a rotocar lands behind her. We turn and a security officer gets out and comes up to us."

"And this wasn't a security ersatz," the news anchor asked. "It was an actual officer, in the flesh?"

"It sure was," the man nodded, "and he didn't waste no time. He pulls out a gun and tells Lulu to move to the rotocar and turn around. We did as he said, then he grabbed our hands and bound them."

The news anchor's face turned from interest to disapproval. "And the officer, he didn't know that Lulu Love was broadcasting?"

"I guess not because he wouldn't a done what he did, if he knew."

"Can you tell us, without going into graphic detail, what happened next?"

"Uh." The man nodded slowly. "Yeah, so, he grabbed us, grabbed Lulu, I mean, and pushed her into the car. She was screaming and hollering that she was broadcasting, but he either didn't hear or thought she was lying. The entire time he's grabbing at her titties and ass. Oh, sorry, can I say titties?"

The news anchor shook his head. "Please continue. When did the security officer realize Lulu was broadcasting?"

"Oh, that was when he yanked her trousers down and slapped his hand on her as—on her derriere. The sensor suit she was wearing is translucent, so he must not have noticed it before. But when he lay hands on it, he knew. The first thing he did was grab his gun and point it at her." The man shook his head. "I honestly, think he would have shot her if she hadn't insisted she was broadcasting live."

The news anchor shook his head again. Samuel also shook himself. This wasn't a killing. This was just some stupid security officer assaulting someone. He slouched back down in his bed and let his heart rate lower. As the news anchor spoke about the uproar this incident had caused, Samuel popped another pani puri into his mouth and think-told Ubiquity to go to the next newscast.

CHAPTER EIGHT: JAGGER JAKOWSKI

It was a long shot, but Jagger was clutching at straws now. To tell Kameke Okonkwo that she'd wasted her money on him wasn't an option. He slurped up the last of the Khao Piak Sen he'd picked up from the Jia Mo Noodle Bar on his way back home. He didn't travel out that way often, which was a shame because it was the best chicken noodle soup in Pherson City. Jagger stood up from his dining table, positioned next to his bed in his one-room apartment, walked the few steps to the kitchen area, and dumped the empty carton in the recycler. He think-told Ubiquity to make him an espresso. The coffee machine whirred into life.

When the rich aroma of java filled his nose, Jagger took the cup from the machine and drank it down in one. The hot liquid burned his throat. A sensation Jagger liked. It woke him up before the caffeine even hit his system. He laughed to himself, thinking how hypocritical he could be, sneering at Xiong for chewing a stimulant leaf, when here he was, drinking coffee, when he could just administer some WideAwake from his endocrine patch.

Jagger picked up his N-Tac suit from his bed and thought about putting it on, but decided against it. He'd just eaten and was feeling bloated. Besides, he didn't actually need to be in immersion to check the meta-data. The dining chair creaked as he dropped into it and placed his hands on the table. He think-told Ubiquity to put his VPN on and bring up Dark Search. Next he commanded it to search for Lana Edge's last immersion. Even though he wasn't in his immersion pod, he could still view the immersion, it would just be a 2D playback projected in front of him. Some immersion studios would record both a 2D and an immersive version of their broadcasts, so people who couldn't afford an immersion pod could still watch via their DigiLenses or a Ubiquity display. Everyone had DigiLenses and a uLink node. The Governance gave them out for free. The deal was, it gave you the ability to access Ubiquity, which you basically needed if you wanted to do anything, and they got data on your every move. Of course you could buy more expensive, better performing DigiLenses or uLink nodes if you could afford to.

The result tile from Dark Search hung in the space above his table. Lana Edge: My Final Immersion. Rather than entering the immersion, Jagger think-told Ubiquity to open its properties. The results tile change to a list of technical items.

Jagger scrolled through the usual things, File Size, File Type, Encoding Process, Raw Header. Nothing stood out as unusual from what he could tell. The Creator field was filled with the name Grace Okonkwo, as expected. He commanded Ubiquity to take the UP number and run a trace on it. Again Grace Okonkwo appeared as the owner.

Jagger sighed. He hadn't really expected to discover anything, even so, the reality was disappointing. Before he quit, Jagger looked over the data again. Everything seemed as it should. Or did it? Under the field 'XUP Toolkit' it said 'XUP Core 9.4.0-l00k-1n5id3'. Jagger didn't understand what 'XUP Toolkit' was, but to him the last part of the entry appeared to say 'look-inside'. Scratching his stubble, Jagger asked Ubiquity to search 'XUP Core 9.4.0-l00k-1n5id3'. Zero results came back for that exact phrase. It looked like someone had edited that entry to leave a message. Look inside. *Look inside what,* Jagger thought.

He stood up, stripped off his clothes, and got into his N-Tac suit. Within a minute he stood in Lana Edge's body in the stairwell of the Ziegler Tower. Jagger think-told Ubiquity to play back the immersion at the slowest speed possible. This was excruciating. The thirty minute immersion was going to take nearly two hours to playback at one frame a second. It also forced Jagger's body to move in slow motion the entire time. But if there was even one frame that would lead to the killer, it would be worth it.

Nearly two hours later, Jagger stumbled out of his immersion pod. He peeled the top of his N-Tac suit down and kicked the chair by his dining table. That had been a painful waste of time. Either the killer was playing with him, or 'XUP Core 9.4.0-l00k-1n5id3' was just some new code, and not a secret message. He was about to quit for the day when he realized he hadn't checked Delilah Dare's immersion. He didn't want to relive her immersion at one frame a second, but he should at least check the meta-data.

Sat at his dining table, Jagger brought up the file.

"Huh."

There it was in the 'XUP Toolkit' field; 'XUP Core 9.4.0-l00k-1n5id3'. He think-told Ubiquity to conduct an additional search on the code but got the same negative result. Jagger scratched his stubble again and wondered what it meant. Look Inside. He'd relived the immersion, scouring it for any clue to the killer, he'd checked the meta-data. Where else could he look? He stood and walked to the windows which covered the entire length of the room.

"Come on Jagger, think."

Out of his ninety-first story apartment window, he had an excellent view of Pherson City. Lines of roto-vehicles flew through the sky between building like orderly insects. His apartment was in a sector full of tall residential towers. He looked across at his neighbors. Most didn't own blinds or anything to stop you from seeing inside their apartments. He'd seen quite a few things he wishes he'd never seen, while staring out his window. Though he couldn't talk. He didn't own blinds either. God knows what his neighbors saw when he was entertaining.

Staring into his neighbor's windows, watching them eating dinner or having sex, Jagger thought inspiration would strike him. Someone would do something that would trigger a eureka moment. But there was nothing.

Jagger gazed vacantly at the apartments opposite. Most were plainly decorated. More a place to sleep than a home. Some citizens, however, appeared to have some pride in where they lived. One couple had decorated their place in bright colors and could be seen making art through the window. Another, obsessed with immersion games, had posters up on his walls of the popular characters.

Jagger's stare kept coming back to his gamer neighbor's apartment. What was it? Games. Immersion games. You could play them, go inside them, but also the game was made, it was produced. It had code inside it.

He shook his head for not thinking of this before. Jagger pulled his N-Tac suit back on and re-entered his immersion pod.

Back in his bubble, Jagger brought up Lana Edge's last immersion. This time, rather than entering the immersion or viewing the meta-data, Jagger opened another program, a file editor. It wasn't the software immersion game designers used to create the games, but it would allow him to see the code that made up the video. Jagger reached out and grabbed Lana Edge's immersion file and placed it into the file editor.

In the space in front of him, a stream of code appeared. The majority of it was gibberish to Jagger, but at the top, beneath the file header, was something he could read. It was a note. A note from the killer.

#

Dear smart person who finds this (if you even exist (I'm starting to doubt it)),

Hello from the stinking lower levels of Pherson City which are filled with the odor of humanity. Hello from the lost, from the faceless (ha ha), hello from the ones you don't care about.

Why did she have to die? Why did she get to live? Why did she get adoration while a million others get nothing? While I get nothing? It turns out you can't walk the sky after all.

It's open within me now. Something inside me that I cannot stop. It will hurt me as well as all the people.

You may find a way to stop the X within, but I cannot.

Yours X, full of woe.
P.S. I guess she really took a fall from Grace.

Jagger stared at the note floating in front of him. He'd done it. He'd found a message from the killer. A sudden flare of excitement lifted his chest. It wasn't often he got a thrill from his work. Jagger shook his head. He didn't want to feel happy. Two women had died. He was a professional. He should be able to carry out his work without letting his emotions come into play. But still, it did feel good.

Jagger copied the note in Grace's file, then closed it. He did a quick search for Delilah Dare's last immersion. When the result tile appeared, he reached out and dragged it over to the file editor program.

The space in front of Jagger filled with code, and right there, beneath the header, was another note.

Hello, is anybody there? Is anyone home?

The stinking gutter of Pherson City laughs at your incompetence. The rat that relies on the discards of society laughs as he takes yet another morsel from in front of your eyes.

Do you not care? Ha! I know the answer to that. Delilah cared. She was a rising star. Now she has risen to the stars. Ha, ha.

Remember, I didn't hate her. It's not me that's doing this. It's you. X is just YOU flowing through me.

Now you know what it's like to die.

Yours X, full of woe.

P.S. I guess she didn't have far to Go.

#

The Pherson City Security station was a brutalist concrete nightmare designed to impose fear in all those that entered it. Even though Jagger was crossing the threshold of his own accord, he experienced the same trepidation he did when being dragged into the station by an officer. The fear that he would not leave again, at least not alive.

The reception desk, separate from the admissions area where the metallic ersatz brought citizens to be booked in, was a petri dish of unsavory life in Pherson City. Jagger sat waiting for Security Officer Collins. Opposite him, a large man stared intensely at Jagger, his bald head covered in dark tattoos. The man's huge hands, dripping in chunky jewelery, rested on his knees. Ready to form a fist at any perceived slight. Jagger wholeheartedly did not want to be on the receiving end of one of their punches.

He brought his gaze down to a small woman perched between the tattooed knucklehead and a man who looked liked he'd taken too much BlissKiss. The small woman looked out of place here. Her aged face, and white hair tied in a bun, along with her modest gray cardigan, over a simple gingham dress looked too sweet, too innocent, to be in the same room as the nodded out junkie and the tattooed knucklehead.

A Ubiquity display on the wall was playing the latest Judge Goode show. Judge Goode was an ex-family court judge who had been hosting an immersive arbitration-based reality court show for years now. In the immersive version you could stand in the body of the plaintiff, defendant or Judge Goode herself, while she listened to the testimonies and questioned the opposing litigants before finally giving her judgment. The show was wildly popular, though Jagger didn't know why. He guessed people loved watching other people's drama. The Ubiquity display was playing back a 2D, non-immersive version of the show.

At the reception counter, someone stared screaming. Jagger glanced over at the scantily clad woman, who thought shouting at the security officer manning the desk would somehow make them do as she commanded. Jagger wasn't sure where to lay his eyes. The woman, who must have been in her early twenties, wore what Jagger thought at first was a short dress with an intricate dark blue pattern on it, that somehow extended down past the edge of the dress hem, by her butt, onto her legs. Jagger frowned. Then, on closer inspection, he realized the blue pattern wasn't on the dress at all. In fact, the dress was made entirely of see-through plastic, and the dark blue pattern was actually a tattoo covering her body. When an electric blue line pulsed through the intricate tattoo, Jagger realized the woman was actually naked under the plastic dress. He chuckled quietly to himself.

It was the heavy breathing that first notified Jagger of the knuckleheads' close proximity. He removed his gaze from the semi-naked tattooed woman and slowly brought it round to the simmering mound of meat that now stood in front of him.

"What you looking at?" the knucklehead said, his voice a low grumble.

Jagger looked slowly up to meet the man's eyes. They were wide and partly covered in a frown that showed Jagger the knucklehead clearly thought he'd done something wrong.

"Just watchin' the world go by," Jagger said. "Nothing more." He had no intention of getting into a fight with this idiot. Especially not in a security station. The knucklehead's meat fists would probably cause some damage before they were both arrested and thrown in a cell.

Jagger's comment was clearly not what the knucklehead had expected to hear. He stood huffing and puffing, his features contorting with what Jagger thought was the effort his tiny brain was going through to come up with a snappy retort.

"Everything okay here?" a voice said from behind Jagger. He recognized it belonged to Security Officer Collins. Jagger swung around and observed the officer he'd spoken to numerous times, but never face to face. The officer had always been controlling an ersatz when they had their encounters.

He was plump, with had kind brown eyes, almost as Jagger imagined, and a black mustache straight out of a different era.

"Ain't nuttin to do with you bacon," the knucklehead said.

"What's going on? You gonna arrest my other brother now?" The tattooed woman from the counter had joined them. "This is harassment. We ain't done jack and you all up in our view. You're scum."

Jagger had to hand it to Collins. The security officer didn't react to the ranting of the nearly naked woman, instead he just stood his ground and smiled.

That Collins could remain calm seemed to infuriate the knucklehead, who clenched his massive meat fists.

"Leave it, Farry," a voice said.

It took Jagger a moment to realize where the words had come from. The knucklehead stepped backwards and Jagger saw it was the little old lady who'd spoken.

"Leave it, he ain't worth it," she spat. Then turning, she slapped the nodded out junkie on the leg, springing him into life. "Come on. Let's get out of this sty."

The little old lady walked out the station exit, followed by the junkie, knucklehead and tattooed women.

"What a charming family," Jagger said, rising to his feet.

"Tell me about it," Collins said before holding out his hand. "Good to meet you, Jagger. What can I do for you?"

Jagger smiled and shook Collins' hand. "Actually, it's what I can do for you."

#

Jagger walked through the security station exit into the windy streets of Pherson City shaking his head. He couldn't believe they weren't taking it seriously. Collins had seemed interested when Jagger had told him what he'd found, but once Captain Rafi got involved things had gone nose dived pretty quickly.

Feeling the chill of the wind, Jagger pulled his collars up and think-told Ubiquity to order him a SkyTaxi. He was well aware that Captain Rafi didn't like him. It started a few years ago when Jagger found a missing boy, the then new Captain had given up on finding. The newscasts had lambasted Pherson City Security significantly, and he thought the captain took it personally.

The descending lights of a rotocar lit the area in front of Jagger. The SkyTaxi landed with a thud and its door automatically opened. He climbed in, noting this SkyTaxi's seats were particularly sticky. If Captain Rafi didn't like Jagger then, he was really going to hate him now. Via Ubiquity, Jagger think-told the SkyTaxi to take him Sector 23. There were numerous immersion studios there, and in one of them he had a contact. A contact that worked on a popular newscast.

Captain Rafi may not have taken the notes he'd found seriously, but he was sure the newscasts and the citizens of Pherson City would. The SkyTaxi rose with a judder and joined a line of rotocars in the orange and red light cast by the perpetual sunset on Viribus B.

CHAPTER NINE: SAMUEL WHEATIES

"Hello from the stinking lower levels of Pherson City, which are filled with the odor of humanity. Hello from the lost, from the faceless, hello from the ones you don't care about." The news anchor turned to face his guest. "Is this honest? Do you believe the killer is actually from the residuum of Pherson City, or is it a ruse to put security off their trail?"

The guest, a stern looking criminal psychologist by the name of Arton Floundry, brought his eyebrows together on his pale face, in what Samuel thought was a well-practiced expression to convey both care and intelligence. As the criminal psychologist opened his mouth to speak, Samuel thinktold ubiquity to change the newscast.

He was semi-lying, semi-sat, on his crusty bed, watching the newscast which floated a few inches above his pudgy belly. Samuel never normally watched the news. It was too full of propaganda, he thought, but when Yuval told him two notes had been discovered, he couldn't resist watching. It was addictive.

It had been a week since the newscasts broke the story about the killer leaving notes. At first there'd been mild concern among the citizens, but with each news report the city had gradually become gripped in a frantic fear of a killer on the loose. He'd been worried now the killer's notes were uncovered, that the final immersions from Lana Edge and Delilah Dare would be removed from the dark Ubiquity. And he was right, they had been. But as soon as they were removed, someone else would upload it again. Even though he felt bad for their deaths, Samuel couldn't help feeling like he was sticking it to the man every time he experienced an immersion the authorities said he shouldn't.

A dark-skinned woman in a vivid green dress hosted the next newscast. She looked out at him with images of Lana Edge and Delilah Dare floating behind her, alongside images of angry people gathered in front of a building.

"—citizens are amassing from all sectors of the city, outside the Security station in protest against the lack of action by Pherson City Security," the news anchor said. "Eum Suk, our Live Vicariously reporter, is on the streets with the protesters. Eum, what's it like there?"

The view changed from the news anchor to a view from the reporter. Showing what he was seeing through his DigiLenses, though it had been cropped into a rectangle frame for the 2D playback Samuel was viewing. He considered pulling his N-Tac suit on and experiencing what the reporter was experiencing in his immersion pod, but he was too comfortable lying down.

The reporter's view was of two women, Samuel guessed were in their twenties, stood in front of the angry citizens.

"Thanks Candy," Eum Suk said, as he turned his head to look over the placard waving crowd. "There is a feeling of frustration and anger in the crowd here. Many are holding signs calling for SerTek Corp, the company that currently has the contract to run Pherson City Security, to be investigated. Other signs simply say, 'protect us'."

Suk returned his gaze back down to the two women in front of him. "I have two protesters here with me. Tell me. Why are you doing this?"

One woman, short blond lady with blue eyes, frowned at Suk. "We're not protesters, we're just citizens. I'm personally here because I've seen story after story of SerTek Corp not care about us residuum. Sure, if an Orinian was in trouble, security's all over it, but us normal citizens? They do nothing. I—"

The short blond woman was cut off by her friend jumping in the conversation. "It's not even that they do nothing. They are actively hurting us. Look what happened the other day when a security officer sexually assaulted that woma—"

The broadcast from the Live Vicariously reporter was abruptly cut and Samuel now stared at the news anchor back in the studio. The one Suk had called Candy.

"...Um... We seem to have lost Eum Suk," Candy said. The image behind her changed from the two murdered LV girls to an older man Samuel vaguely recognized. "There have been calls from activist groups for Viribus B Coordinator Wei Gao to intervene and bring Governance Force Investigators in. So far the Viribus B Coordinator's office has declined to comment."

Samuel think-told Ubiquity to change newscasts. A group of people were sitting around a black glass table.

"Is it time for SerTek Corp lost their contract to run Pherson City security?" one man said. "Some are calling for the security force to be run by the city, and not by a private entity."

A gruff-looking man in a sharp suit shook his head. "SerTek doesn't just run Pherson City Security, they ar—"

Samuel think-told Ubiquity to change newscasts. He'd exhausted the regular mainstream newscasts and was now viewing one of the more outlandish channels, and he could tell. The news anchor on this channel, KOS News, looked like someone they'd pulled in off the street, rather than the overly slick presenters on the other newscasts. Samuel kind of liked that. It made him seem more relatable. The news anchor spoke with a man in an outlandish white and blood red robe, with a band tied around his head and his features twisted in an intense visage. As he talked, the man waved his arms, making the many beads at his wrists clank together.

"You need to understand Murray, X is doing this for us. It is a gift. H—"

"Grandmaster Vonhoff, how is killing innocent LV girls a gift?" Murray Murnaghan, the news anchor, said. The serious frown on his face incongruent with bizarre outfit the other man wore.

Grandmaster Vonhoff's face went hard, his eyes wild. "Have you done it? Have you experienced death?"

Murray looked down to his feet. Samuel guessed he was considering whether to tell the truth of not. He shook his head.

"Well, you should," the crazed robed man continued. "X has allowed us to experience death. To experience death is to cleanse your soul. That is the gift. Look at the last words in his notes. Grace and Go. They are not random. Grace is a spiritual gift that involves love and mercy given to others, even when we feel they don't deserve it.

"Go means to start. So, X is telling us we must start from a place of love and mercy. He wants us to understand what the residuum of Pherson City goes through. To understand that everyday they die. They die over and over again to keep the gears of the Governance turning.

"When X said 'It's not me that's doing this. It's you. X is just YOU flowing through me.' He's showing us he doesn't want to kill, but is simply reenacting what the Governance does. It kills its citizens so that others can thrive."

The look on the news anchor's face changed from serious to shock. "I'm sorry Grandmaster Vonhoff, but I have t—"

Grandmaster Vonhoff stood up and spread his arms. "Do not be sorry. The time has come. Experience death. Cleanse your soul. You wil—"

Murray Murnaghan stood up and moved in front of Grandmaster Vonhoff. "I have breaking news. There has been a new killing. Another Live Vicariously creator has been killed. This time it's a man. A man called Harry Hard."

Grandmaster Vonhoff said something, but Samuel didn't hear him. His mind leaped out of its sedentary state and became alert. A new killing. This is what he'd been waiting for. Samuel frantically scrambled off his bed, sliding to the floor in the process. He stood up. A tingle rushed through his mind as his heart raced. He reached down and grabbed his N-Tac suit, but as he yanked it up, it got stuck on something. He yanked again, but it didn't budge. Samuel realized he was standing on the N-Tac suit. He moved his foot and took a breath, realizing he nearly broke it. And then what would he do? He couldn't afford a new one.

Samuel took another deep breath, filling his

lungs with air that smelled of stale sweat and old food. He closed his eyes. Grandmaster Vonhoff was right. This was a gift. He shouldn't rush into it, he should savor it. He'd begged himself not to, but it'd been a long two weeks waiting for a fresh death. A new chance to cleanse his soul. Yes. He liked that expression.

With a sense of calm, Samuel took a moment to inquire via Ubiquity who Grandmaster Vonhoff was. A summary appeared in the air in front of him. Grandmaster Vonhoff, whose real name was Derek Vonhoff, was an ex-Lumen facilitator, who had formed a cult-like quasi-religious group called the Life Through Death. They advocated the use of the Lumen sacrament Egosh as an opportunity to be reborn.

Samuel's jaw dropped open. Life Through Death. That was exactly what he felt he was experiencing when he relived Lana or Delilah's deaths. Torn between wanting to relive this fresh death and wanting to find out more about Life Through Death, Samuel stood conflicted. Finally, he pulled his N-Tac suit on over his pudgy, naked body. He'd find out all about Life Through Death. But not before he stepped into the body of Harry Hard to experience the thrill of his final moments. To experience his death. To cleanse his soul.

CHAPTER TEN: JAGGER JAKOWSKI

Jagger stared down into Creamy Pie's hazel eyes. Even though she was tied to the bed posts with a gag in her mouth, she didn't look scared. In fact her gold-flecked eyes were alive under her brows, which curved upwards in ecstasy. He thrust again, arching his body into hers, then glanced towards the mirror so everyone could see the beast with two backs.

Jagger hated this. Killer X's latest victim was a Live Vicariously creator named Harry Hard who specialized in erotic experiences. The killing had taken place while Harry Hard was performing with Creamy Pie, another erotic Live Vicariously creator. The two worked together often, giving their fans the opportunity to experience the sexual acts they performed from either body. This type of immersion didn't turned Jagger on. In fact, being forced to live each of these experiences made him feel violated. When Jagger had discovered what Harry Hard was doing when the murder happened, he'd nearly decided not to view it in immersion, but his desire to be professional, not to miss a single clue, had driven him to do it. Now here he was, several minutes into the act, and he perversely prayed for Harry Hard's death to happen soon.

Harry Hard turned away from the mirror. They bent forward and kissed Creamy Pie on her gagged lips, then worked their kisses down onto her neck. The background music was loud and energetic with the trench-beat that was popular. Jagger felt Creamy Pie's body tighten around them. Harry Hard didn't seem to notice. He must have thought she was reacting to his stimulation, but with the hindsight Jagger brought to experience, he knew this must be the moment the killing began.

Creamy Pie screamed through her gag and thrashed her head from side to side. Jagger, with Harry, lifted his face from her neck and stared into Creamy Pie's eyes. This time, the look in them was unmistakable. Fear.

There was a pause while Harry Hard reacted to her. He didn't know why she'd made that face. Jagger thought maybe Harry Hard was concerned it was something he'd done.

Harry Hard stopped thrusting and said, "What's wro—"

A strap looped over Harry Hard's head so quickly he barley saw it. It tightened and Harry Hard's body tensed with the shock of being strangled. To Jagger, the tightening around the neck, even though it wouldn't be fatal through his N-Tac suit, was sickening when combined with being forced to carry out Harry Hard's final movements.

After a second of disbelief, Harry Hard stared to fight back. His hands came up to the strap around his neck. His fingers tried to work some space between the material and his skin, but the killer just tightened the strap further.

They opened their mouth and screamed. Then Jagger realized the scream only came from him, echoing around inside his immersion pod. Harry Hard's mouth was open, but no sound escaped.

Harry Hard tried to push the killer off his back, but the weight was too heavy. Desperately he tried to swing a fist upwards to hit his attacker, but all that did was make him lose his balance. As soon as his fist moved up, he fell forwards and smacked his head into Creamy Pie's face.

Staring into the pillow, Harry Hard stopped struggling and a moment later everything flashed white and Jagger floated in the center of his tile bubble. He exited the immersion pod into his apartment and clawed the N-Tac suit down off his neck. Sweat dripped from his forehead as he stood bent over, panting. None of the Live Vicariously deaths had been pleasant, but this one made Jagger feel physically sick.

He peeled the rest of the N-Tac suit off and staggered the short distance to his shower. Cold water rained down on Jagger, as he stood trying to convince his body it wasn't him that died. It wasn't him that had just experienced that trauma. But his body knew a lie. It flooded Jagger system with adrenaline and cortisol, making his heart pound. Jagger let his body slide down to the shower floor. He'd meant to experience Creamy Pie's version of the incident straight after, but he knew now that would not happen. Then, as the intensity of the adrenaline rush faded, Jagger's brain started to work again. He think-told Ubiquity to administer some KeepCalm. The endocrine patch on his arm whirred, and a second later small dose of benzodiazepine entered Jagger's system. A calmness wash over him. Shortly he'd administer some

CoConfidence, but for the moment, Jagger was content to sit in silence and let the stress grip release him. This wasn't the first immersion death he'd experienced, but this time he'd really felt like he'd died vicariously.

#

Harry Hard pressed himself into Jagger's inner thighs, then bent forward and kissed him. In real life Jagger had shared a bed with a man, though there'd always been at least one woman in the mix of bodies. Now, living a sexual experience through Creamy Pie, he felt both vulnerable and uncomfortable. He tried to phase out the physical sensations and focus on anything that might give away the identity of the killer.

As Harry Hard continued to thrust into them, Jagger looked for the first sign of the killer's entry. It was difficult as he was forced to look at whatever Creamy Pie was stared at, which invariably was Harry Hard. His chiseled face and light brown hair were getting sweaty with the exertion. Harry rotated his torso to peer at himself in a mirror set up next to her bed. And while Creamy Pie was still focusing on Harry Hard's muscled body for her fans to enjoy, the intensity for Jagger eased a little, allowing him to look at the bedroom in her peripheral vision. He'd inspected the room at the beginning of the immersion, before Creamy Pie and Harry Hard had begun their performance. From what Jagger could ascertain by the size, it was located in an affluent sector of Pherson City. Obviously being a Live Vicariously creator paid off, well, for some it did anyway. A soft light lit the bedroom taking the hard edges off the little furniture. The walls were painted to a pale color and were plain apart from a single abstract painting hung above the bed. At the foot of the bed the door sat closed, to the left a wardrobe covered the length of the wall, with the mirror stood in front of it. The opposite wall was entirely glass, like so many of the tall residential buildings in Pherson City, giving views of the forest of skyscrapers and the lights of rotocar lanes that dissected them. Creamy Pie had been careful to start her immersion in her bedroom, so not to show anyone viewing where she lived, or so she thought. Jagger knew it wouldn't take him long to workout from the view which building they were located in. And if he could, so could the killer.

Harry Hard leaned forward and kissed them. Jagger knew it wasn't long now. Harry Hard's kisses made their way down to Creamy Pie's neck, and that's when he saw it. The bedroom door opened and a dark figure walked in. Creamy Pie tensed her body around Harry Hard. Jagger think-told Ubiquity to freeze the playback. There it was. The best view of the killer yet. The bedroom's soft light was just enough to activate the reflective parts of the otherwise black outfit. From their size, Jagger guessed it was most likely a man. They wore the same black hooded jacket, trousers, and boots as before. Gloves covered his hands, which meant finger prints were a no-go. And he wore the same face mask with the red X on it. In his immersion pod, Jagger breathed out heavily. There was no new information for him to go on. Annoyed, he restarted the playback.

Creamy Pie thrashed her head back and forth, trying to alert Harry Hard of the killer's presence. Meanwhile, the killer moved to the bed and pulled something out of his pocket. It looked like a lanyard. Harry Hard lifted his face away from Creamy Pie's neck and stared at her with a puzzled expression. Seeing the genuine worry in his features, not for his own safety, but for his co-performer, was heartbreaking. The look lasted only a second before the killer looped the lanyard over Harry Hard's neck and pulled it tight.

Harry's body tensed on top of Jagger's and Creamy Pie's, as the shock of being strangled swept across his body. For what seemed like seconds, Harry Hard did nothing. He stared at Creamy Pie with a look of disbelief, then his hands came up to his neck, desperately trying to pry the lanyard away from his skin.

Tightness pulled on Jagger's wrists and ankles as Creamy Pie struggled against the bindings that held her to the bed. His heart pounded as she struggled to free herself to help Harry Hard, all while staring into her friend's now purple face, his eyes bulging with fear and the lack of oxygen.

Harry Hard gave up trying to get the lanyard off his neck and opted to hit his attacker. But as soon as he raised a fist backwards to strike out, the weight of the attacker forced him forwards. Harry Hard's face smashed into Creamy Pie's causing Jagger to flinch in his immersion pod. He thought nothing would have been worse than experiencing Harry Hard's death first hand, but he was wrong. This was worse. Harry Hard's body jerked and twitched as he tried to fight back, then heartbreakingly the twitching stopped as the life drained from his body. Jagger, along with Creamy Pie, stared upwards at the killer looming over them. Annoyingly, the close proximity revealed nothing new. The red X stared down at them with the same cold lack of expression. Harry Hard had stopped moving, but the killer kept the lanyard tight around his neck. He obviously wanted to make sure he finished the job.

Creamy Pie started sobbing. Jagger, too, felt a deep sense of sadness and despair wash over him. The killer climbed off the bed. The lifeless body of Harry Hard lay heavily on Creamy Pie and Jagger. Jagger was ready to exit the immersion when the killer walked to the bedroom door and there was a brief white flash. It was attached to the lanyard. The killer opened the door and left.

Jagger think-told Ubiquity to rewind and paused the immersion at the point just before the killer exited. There it was. Gripped in the killer's fist was the lanyard, and hanging from the lanyard was a white rectangle with a code pattern. *Bingo,* thought Jagger.

#

The glass of beer was cool in Jagger's hand. He drank half a pint down in two thirsty gulps. It had been a long time since he'd needed a beer so badly. He placed the glass on the counter of Le Petit Zinc and tried to stifle the burp that rose from his stomach. In front of him, Lolo, the owner of the bar, stood shaking her head.

"You look like something ze cat dragged in."

"I've had better days," Jagger said before taking another swig of his drink. "How long until Collins comes by?"

Lolo stared into space for a moment, then refocused on Jagger. "He should go by any moment now. But if zis clue is so good, why don't you go to the station?"

Jagger slid off the barstool and walked to the exit. Multicolored lights from the ceiling danced over his body, onto the floor off in a circular motion, highlighting how empty Le Petit Zinc was at this time of day.

"Yeah," he said turning back to Lolo, "they probably wouldn't be too happy to see my face."

Lolo shook her head again, but said nothing as he tuned and stepped out into the windy, perpetual sunset of Pherson City. Few citizens were around, and those who were had their jacket collars pulled tight around their heads. The difference in temperature between the side of Viribus B that was locked to the star, and the side that always faced away, created constant winds that circled the planet. Jagger popped his collar up and looked along the street. This sector was full of bars and restaurants, but as most residents of Viribus B followed Earth Standard time, they'd be at work right now. This left the street, which normally bubbled with life empty and rather sad looking. It did, however, make it easy to spot Collins, or at least the ersatz he controlled.

One hundred meters away, the metallic machine stomped along the center of the street, its chrome body catching the neon lights of the various establishments. Jagger didn't know what to think of these on the ground ersatz patrols. He was old enough to remember when SerTek Corp took over the contract to provide security for Pherson City. They'd welcomed them in, as the previous company had become corrupt, and was essentially an extension of the main organized crime syndicate that ran the city back then. Some saw the ersatz patrols introduced by SerTek Corp as a heavy-handed approach, which when you considered the fire power they housed, you could understand. But it had worked and slowly the streets of Pherson City were reclaimed from the gangs. It was far from an idyllic paradise, but the extra force, plus the Governance funding of programs to offer ex-gang members other options in life, had pulled the city from the verge of descent into chaos. But that had been long ago, and now SerTek Corp itself was seen as a bloated, self-serving organization, that allowed enough crime to exist so it could request more money each year.

Jagger watched as the menacing machine approached him. It's featureless face, that of a cold killer if it chose to be.

"You've got some nerve, Jakowski," Collins' voice said from the metal beast.

Jagger glanced at a woman dressed in a gray kimono and khaki trousers with boots too big for her as she walked by.

"I took the notes to Pherson City Security first," Jagger said. "Not my fault if Captain Rafi is too full of himself to take it seriously."

The ersatz straightened and raised its arm. Jagger knew this was a threat. Inside that arm was enough firepower to disintegrate him.

"Whoa," Jagger said, holding his hands up. "Come on Collins. I'm trying to do the same thing as you. Make this city a safe place." When no sound came from the ersatz, Jagger continued. "Look, I've viewed the latest immersion the killer posted on the dark Ubiquity. At the end, you can see a code on the card attached to the lanyard the killer used. I ran a search. The code is for a maintenance operative called Boone Jaenke. A really nasty piece of work judging by his rap sheet. I thi—"

"How did you do a search on his code card?

He's a Governance contractor. Only Governance systems should be able to decode the card."

Jagger shrugged as the wind picked up, making a whistling sound as it found its way along the lifeless street. "You'd be surprised what you can find out on the dark Ubiquity. That's not the point though. The point is the killer might be Boone Jaenke, or someone who could take his access card."

Collins was silent for a moment. A rotocar flew by in the air above, its landing lights slid over the chrome body of the ersatz. "This is none of your business, Jakowski. I suggest you stay out of it."

The ersatz moved forwards stomping down, Jagger had to step out of the way to avoid being crushed.

"If SerTek doesn't look into this, I'll go to the newscasts again," Jagger shouted out to the back of the security machine. The ersatz stopped in its tracks ten meters away and turned around. Jagger gulped. He knew saying that would get Collins' attention, but he didn't know how pissed off it would make him. The ersatz stomped the ten meters between them terrifyingly fast and now stood over Jagger. If Collins wanted to kill him, he wouldn't even need to use any of the weapons housed in the ersatz's body. At this proximity, he could snap his neck with a flick of the metallic beast's wrist.

Jagger instinctively shrank back. His survival instinct taking over from any bravado he might have thought he had. The ersatz bent forward, so it loomed over Jagger.

"Not that it's any of your business, but we know about Jaenke," Collins said, anger clear in his voice. "But it looks like he has an alibi. After that shit you pulled with the newscasts, we're all over this. What we don't need is some jackass armchair vigilante screwing up our investigation. Understand?"

The humanoid killing machine stared down at Jagger. He caught a glimpse of himself in its featureless, shiny black head. It shocked him. He could clearly see the fear in his own face. The security ersatz straightened, turned, and stomped away, leaving Jagger alone with the wind.

CHAPTER ELEVEN: SAMUEL WHEATIES

The rusty elevator door opened and Samuel stepped into a scene he didn't have the energy to deal with right now.

"What's wrong with you?" Geraldina said, standing over Yuval, who was on his knees, picking up garbage scattered across the corridor. "Why'd you have no respect for our apartments?"

Yuval looked up at Samuel as he approached. The small man's wrinkled face held frustration that was bubbling over into anger.

"Can you tell that old hag that I didn't make this mess, I'm just clearing it up. It was probably those delinquents, who run around here all the time."

"He would say that," Geraldina said, turning to Samuel. "If he'd been caught."

Samuel sighed as he squeezed his large frame past his two bickering neighbors. He didn't have time for this. While he'd been working, the news broke that another LV creator had been killed. In the week since Harry Hard's death, Samuel had become obsessed with the Life Through Death group. Their message of Experience Death, Cleanse Your Soul, had resonated with him so much that he'd spent every waking minute either listening to Grandmaster Vonhoff's speeches, or viewing Life Through Death's guided version of the LV death immersions. Whereas before he was becoming jaded by reliving them, experiencing the deaths while listening Grandmaster Vonhoff preach, had lifted the whole thing to another level. Now it wasn't about getting sexual kicks, though that was still part of it, now it was also something bigger, now it was a journey, a pathway to salvation. With Grandmaster Vonhoff, he experienced death, and he cleansed his soul.

"I heard another one of those LV creators got killed," Yuval said as Samuel went past. "I hope you've stopped obsessing about them. You need to get outside and do things with your life."

Samuel paused at the door to his apartment. He considered turning back and telling Yuval about Life Through Death, but the old man would never understand. Instead, he looked at his entry system. The Ubiquity recorder recognized his face, and the door clicked as it unlocked. He pushed it open and went inside. As he shut the door behind him, he heard Geraldina begin be berate her neighbor again. Samuel was glad he wasn't Yuval.

#

Hundreds of tiles surrounded Samuel, glimmering with previews of immersions. Floating in the center of his bubble, he quickly discarded his notification tiles and opened dark Ubiquity. He swiped through until he found Life Through Death's immersions. The tiles in front of him changed to display the latest immersions Grandmaster Vonhoff had released. Samuel considered immediately experiencing the death as the killer had uploaded it, but after spending almost every waking hour of the previous week in the Life Through Death immersions, he felt it would be wrong to experience this new death, without Grandmaster Vonhoff there to augment the event with his wisdom.

Samuel felt his heart jump when he saw the latest immersion. The tile was a flickering wall of flames with the title, Through Fire We Rise Again Reborn. A tingling sensation, nothing to do with the N-Tac suit, rippled over Samuel's body. He think-told Ubiquity to take him in and everything flashed white.

He found himself stood at the bottom of an enormous staircase as wide as the eye could see. The steps were white and glowed softly, as if cast in a heavenly light. Behind him, white clouds pushed him forward to the stairs. Samuel stepped up onto the first step and was astonished how easily he could move. It was like walking on air. He continued to step upward through the paradisaical glow when he saw him. Grandmaster Vonhoff stood a few feet above, his white and blood red rode softened by the light. He smiled when he saw Samuel and held out a hand. Samuel reached up to take it, but Grandmaster Vonhoff moved on before he could make contact. For a second Samuel had forgotten this was a recording. His heart dropped. A feeling of foolishness swept over him. The cloud behind Samuel forced him upwards alongside Grandmaster Vonhoff, who turned to him and said, "It's good to see you, brother."

"It's good to see you too, Grandmaster Vonhoff. I have waited for the day when I can exp—"

"Killer X has given us something special today," Grandmaster Vonhoff's recoding said. As they walked, Vonhoff turned his smiling, gentle face towards Samuel. "You know, it's not just individuals that produce Live Vicariously immersions, organization also do."

Samuel knew this, but he'd no interest in living through what was essentially advertisement for a company. They continued to climb.

"Yes, killer X has shown us something truly special. It is the ultimate symbol of life through death."

As they climbed up, Samuel noticed the stairs were losing their soft white glow. In fact, the higher they climbed, the darker they got. Until they were walking on steps made of gray ash that seemed to crumble behind them as their foot lifted from it.

"What's happening?" Samuel said to the Grandmaster.

Grandmaster Vonhoff continued walking up the steps as if Samuel hadn't spoken. Then, in the gloomy gray glow ahead of them, Samuel saw something. At first it was just a small dark smear in the distance above. But as they approached, its edges became defined and he could see it was a door. A door stood alone on the stairs. No wall on either side, just more stairs. Samuel swallowed. This wasn't the usual way Grandmaster Vonhoff conducted his guided Live Vicariously immersions. Normally they just spoke in a plain void and then everything would flash white and you'd be in the LV creator's body, with Grandmaster Vonhoff's disembodied voice speaking to you. Explaining to you the significance of what was happening. This was different. And it thrilled Samuel.

They arrived at the door, and Grandmaster Vonhoff turned to Samuel and smiled softly.

"What you are about to experience will change your life. This may be the hardest one yet killer X has given us, but do not fear. I will be there with you." Grandmaster Vonhoff opened the door, revealing a wall of flames. They twitched and danced, and Samuel could feel the intense heat coming off of them. "Go ahead and experience rebirth. Experience life through death."

Samuel didn't move, but the immersion

pushed him forwards towards the door. For a half-second he considered telling Ubiquity to exit the immersion, but the longer he stared at the flames, the more hypnotic they became, until they immersed him and the door shut behind him.

CHAPTER TWELVE: JAGGER JAKOWSKI

"No fracking way," Jagger said. He shook his head, making the newscast he was viewing through his DigiLenses dance about the room. He sat at the table in his small studio apartment, in utter disbelief at how stupid Pherson City Security could be.

The newscasts were full of the news. They had caught Killer X. Captain Rafi's recorded message, from the steps of Pherson City Security station, was on all the channels. His self-satisfied face, beaming with smugness that got Jagger's back right up. He grabbed the fork he'd been eating with and threw it at the captain's face. The fork went through the image of the newscast and clanked into the metal drop-off box attached to his window that drones used to deliver packages. *How can they be so dumb,* Jagger thought?

Pherson City Security hadn't caught the supposed killer, someone by the name of Donny Zaytsev. No, this guy actually walked right through the front door and surrendered. Said he couldn't live with what he'd done. And Captain Rafi and his idiot underlings ate that crap up.

Now Captain Rafi's arrogant face was on every newscast, saying Pherson City Security was the best in all the Governance. It made Jagger's blood boil. Just looking at Donny Zaytsev, you could tell this guy was full of merde. He was a sad, lonely man, but he wasn't the killer. He just wanted attention, and that idiot Captain Rafi was giving it to him.

A call notification flashed up in Jagger's vision. It was from Kameke Okonkwo. Jagger think-told Ubiquity to answer the call on his wall display so they could both view each other. He turned to the wall just as Kameke Okonkwo's image appeared.

"God don butter my bread, thank you Cit Jakowski," Kameke Okonkwo said, her face held in a mix of rejoice and sorrow.

"Cit Okonkwo," Jagger said, holding up a hand. "I didn't do this."

Kameke Okonkwo smiled and shook her head. "The pressure you put on Pherson City Security. That felt across the city. Without that, I don't think him coming forward."

"No, no," Jagger said, sitting up straighter in his chair. "I don't think Zaytsev is the killer."

"What?" A frown fell across Kameke Okonkwo's face.

"Just that. I don't think Donny Zaytsev killed Grace, or Delilah Dare. I think he just wants attention."

"But, but Security say him do it."

Jagger could see the doubt and pain spread through Kameke Okonkwo's mind, and he felt awful. Just when she thought she had resolution, he was taking it all away.

"Cit Okonkwo. I'm going to keep on investigating this. Okay?"

Kameke Okonkwo's face looked troubled. "Okay. If you say so."

"I'll be in touch soon," Jagger said, then cut the call. The newscast he was watching automatically started again in his vision.

Annoyed, Jagger think-told Ubiquity to stop the newscast and instead show him the notes killer X had left in the metadata, starting with Harry Hard's. He had to get to the bottom of this. For Kameke Okonkwo's sake.

A white rectangle lit up the space in front of Jagger with the note.

Hello again, heartless world.

If you cared you would have stopped X by now. But X is just growing and growing. And you sicken me. You don't want this to stop. You eat it up like X eats the lives of these innocent citizens.

Why did Harry Hard need to die? If you haven't figured it out yet maybe you never will. What will I do? What's taking you so long? We're running out of days.

Yours X, my mother always said I was Wednesday's.

P.S. Harry hard was loving and Giving.

Jagger scratched his head. What did the killer mean? We're running out of days? His mother always said he's Wednesday's. What the hell did that mean? Harry Hard was loving and giving. Was that because it was an erotic LV creator?

Jagger cursed himself for not being good at riddles. Then he remembered Captain Rafi's smug face, and that no one else had figured it out yet either. Hell, he might be the only one still investigating the case.

He think-told Ubiquity to display the next note. This killing had been different. Rather than killing a normal Live Vicariously creator, killer X had slaughtered a Pherson City Fire Fighter. Jafari Okeke was his name. He'd worked for the fire department for a little over a year and had only just become their Live Vicariously representative. Lots of companies and organizations would do this, ask one recently employed person to wear a sensor suit and go about their day, so normal citizens could see what it was like.

For Pherson City Fire Department, this was meant to show the difficulty of their job, and also show people the dangers of fires and how they are caused.

Reliving Okeke's death had been the worse one

yet for Jagger to experience. Far worse than Harry Hard's. The killer had started a fire at a warehouse. He clearly knew how Pherson City Fire Department and Okeke operated, because he started one big fire that drew the attention of the majority of the firefighters, and a smaller fire in a side office that Okeke would deal with. This was fairly standard. Even though Pherson City Fire Department wanted to show how they dealt with fires, they didn't want to put Okeke in actual danger.

When Okeke stepped into the room, he saw behind the fire a giant red X spray painted on the wall, and beneath it the words; You work so hard for a living.

Barely two seconds later, the entire room ignited and engulfed Okeke in flames. Jagger shuddered as he recalled Okeke's screams as he burned to death.

Trying to bury the experience deep in his mind, Jagger focused on the note floating in front of him.

Is it getting hot in here or is it just me?

The festering streets of Pherson City are not shocked. They know you don't care. They know you are pathetic. You only care for yourself. Who cares what happens to other people? Not you.

It's nearly over. If you don't stop X I'll have to find another game to play.

Yours X, full of woe, not long to go.

P.S. Okeke worked hard for a Living (come on, what more do you need?)

Jagger's head hurt. He stood and walked to his window looking out at the other apartment buildings. A scattered set of lights on the buildings showed him the majority of his neighbors were still at work. He leaned his forehead on the cool glass. The killer was clearly annoyed that no one had figured out his code. If there was a code. So maybe he'd decided to hand himself in? Maybe Donny Zaytsev was the killer? The notes said he was full of woe, after all. Maybe this was the other game killer X said he'd have to play?

Jagger smacked the window. It just didn't feel right. *My mother always said I was Wednesday's.* What did that mean? Jagger didn't know. What he did know was that his body felt disgusting. He kicked off his boots and walked to the shower, discarding items of clothing as he went.

In the shower the jets came at him from all four walls, the heat stinging his skin. He think-told Ubiquity to run message program one. The jets changed into pulsing waves. Jagger closed his eyes and placed his palms on the wall above him, letting the undulating torrents knead the tension out of his muscles.

He kept repeating parts of the notes in his head as the water smashed into him. *Grace. I guess she didn't have far to Go. My mother always said I was Wednesday's. Yours X, full of woe.*

Jagger opened his eyes. He knew this.

"Something, something, have to go. Wednesday's something was full of woe." Jagger slammed his palm into the shower wall. *I know this, what is it!*

Then, for a nanosecond, his mind cleared and delivered him the answer.

He stood taller in the shower, and a memory from his youth appeared. His mother was perched on a chair, telling him a nursery rhyme.

"Monday's child is fair of face. Tuesday's child is full of grace. Wednesday's child is full of woe. Thursday's child has far to go. Friday's child is loving and giving. Saturday's child works hard for a living. And the child born on the Sabbath day, is fair and wise and good in every way."

Smiling, Jagger exited the shower. The water automatically shut off as he stepped out. That was it. The post scripts in each note ended with a capitalized word. Grace, Go, Giving and Living. They matched the last word in each line in the nursery rhyme. All apart from Monday, Wednesday and Sunday, the Sabbath day.

Jagger grabbed a towel and pulled it over his skin absentmindedly as he walked back to his living area. Wednesday's child is full of woe. That's what the killer said he was. Full of woe. There was one missing. Monday. Jagger threw the towel on his unmade bed and sat naked on the chair by the table.

He think-told Ubiquity to show news reports of Live Vicariously creators killed in the last year. Apart from Lana Edge, Delilah Dare, Harry Hard and Jafari Okeke, there had been none.

"Goddamn it." He was sure he'd find another LV death. One that would link to Monday's child is fair of face. Jagger kicked the table in frustration. "Ouch." He pulled his unclad foot up onto to his other leg and inspected it for damage. *That's it.*

He think-told Ubiquity to show any news reports of Live Vicariously creators who'd been injured in the last six months. A long list of results appeared. It turned out LV creators were hurting themselves all the time, with their ever-increasing antics to gain attention.

He scanned through the list. He wasn't sure what he was looking for, but he was sure he'd know it when he saw it. And he was right. After scrolling back only a few weeks, there it was. Addison Daly. He was a beauty LV creator. From what Jagger could tell, he used his status as a LV creator to be sent free cosmetics and clothing, which he'd then rave about in his immersions. The news report said in one of his immersions, when he was testing out some sportswear a company had sent him, someone had thrown acid in his face. Pherson City Security never arrested anyone and put it down to a jealous fan.

Monday's child is fair of face.

Jagger pushed himself up from his chair, pulled on his N-Tac suit, and entered his immersion pod.

Everything flashed white and Jagger wasted no time by immediately starting up his VPN and bringing up Dark Search. It only took him a few seconds of searching to find Addison Daly's last immersion. Jagger opened the file editor, reached out a hand, grabbed the immersion and threw it into the file editor. There it was. In-between the file header and the gibberish of the code, a new note appeared. The first note the killer had sent.

So it begins,

I come from the dark unseen cracks in Pherson City. The places you avoid, the places you ignore. The festering stench of humanity that the Governance only cares about when it stops being productive.

X runs through me. X sees the pain. Now you must know the pain. And ah! The wonder of technology. Isn't it great? Now you too can live through the moment when someone loses everything.

Addison Daly only cared about himself. He represents all of you in the Governance. Looking in the mirror as you stand on the heads of those in the gutters. So relive it and see.

X runs through me and cannot be stopped (not by little old me anyway). Next time he won't be so nice.

Yours X, full of woe.
P.S. Addison Daly WAS fair of face.

Jagger copied the note out and closed the file editor. He floated in the center of his bubble for a moment, feeling numb. The killer had been leaving clues this whole time, and no one had noticed. All those Live Vicariously creators might still be alive if he'd worked this out earlier. Jagger shook his head. There was no point in feeling despondent. That wouldn't help, especially when there was one day left. The sabbath day.

"And the child born on the Sabbath day, is fair and wise and good in every way."

Jagger exited his immersion pod and stripped off his N-Tac suit. For the first time in the entire investigation, Jagger felt like he knew what was happening. The killer had said they were running out of days. Now he knew there was only one left, and he was sure he knew who the victim would be.

#

"You can't go in there," the young studio assistant said, as Jagger pushed his way through a doorway lit by a sign that said; On Air.

"Hey!"

Jagger strode into a courtroom. Either side of him, in the benches of the public gallery, the audience of extras turned and stared. Some whispered under their breaths, clearly excited to see the new direction this episode of Judge Goode was taking. Ahead of him, Judge Goode sat behind a caramel colored wooden bench, while the two litigants stood at small tables in front of her. The litigant speaking fell silent and twisted round to see what the commotion was.

"What is this?" Judge Goode said. Jagger noticed her glance sideways to the bailiff. The eyes of the actor who played the bailiff widened, but his body remained rigid.

"Judge Goode, I'm here to warn you," Jagger said, as he stepped through the swing door in the barrier between the audience and the litigants. "You're in danger."

The two litigants backed away from Jagger to either side of the faux courtroom. Whatever petty dispute they held against each other melted away as the energy in the faux courtroom turned from excitement to fear.

"What are you talking about?" Judge Goode said, standing up in her judge's bench.

"Killer X," Jagger said as he approached the bench. "You're going to be his next victim."

Judge Goode scrambled back from Jagger, clearly thinking Jagger was the killer. Behind him, the courtroom doors burst open and two private security officers entered, guns raised.

"Get down on the floor," one officer said.

Jagger glanced back at the officers and raised his hands. "It's not like that. Judge Goode, look at the notes. Monday's Child is fair of face. Tuesday's child i—"

"On the floor!"

Jagger slowly lowered himself to the floor.

The two private security officers made quick work of binding Jagger's hands behind his back and getting him to his feet. The Live Vicariously immersion was still broadcasting after all. As they led him through the audience gallery, Jagger took one last stab at warning Judge Goode.

"And the child born on the sabbath day, is fair and wise and good in every wa—"

The last word was cut short when one of the private security officers punched Jagger in the kidney.

CHAPTER THIRTEEN: SAMUEL WHEATIES

Samuel laughed as he watched Jagger Jakowski being dragged from the courtroom. He popped a salsa laden chip into his mouth as the scene projected above his belly changed from Judge Goode's immersion, to a shot of Jakowski sat in a chair in the newscast studio. The news anchor, Murray Murnaghan, turned to face Jakowski.

"So, you really believe Judge Goode is in danger?"

"Yes," Jakowski said, shuffling in his seat, clearly uncomfortable being in a broadcast. "The final line of the nursery rhyme says, fair and wise and good in every way. If you look at the other days mentioned, they all match the postscripts in the notes the killer left."

"We're not doubting that Cit Jakowski." Murray Murnaghan turned to face the recorder with a barely contained smirk. "I'm just wondering how Donny Zaytsev will get to Judge Goode, when he's locked up in a cell in the Sector 8 Detention

Center?"

Jagger shook his head. "As I said, Donny Zaytsev isn't the killer. If you'd just liste—"

"Yes, yes," Murray Murnaghan said over Jakowski. "We know. Pherson City Security are incompetent. Okay everyone, we need to break for a quick commercial but stay with us, as next we have a guest that claims he can prove the lovable kids character, Lenny Lima, is a satanic symbol used by devil worshipers. Don't go anywhere now."

Murray Murnaghan's smiling face vanished as Samuel think-told Ubiquity to stop the playback. He swung his legs off the bed and got to his feet, shaking his head.

"That Jakowski is such an idiot."

Samuel brushed the chip crumbs off his chest and checked his hair in the mirror. "Everyone knows the proper end to the nursery rhyme is; And the child born on the sabbath day, is bonny and blithe, and good and gay."

The door to his apartment slammed shut as Samuel strode down the corridor to work.

#

Samuel slammed the door to his apartment and threw his jacket to the floor. His t-shirt clipped his ears as he pulled it off, balled it up and launched it at a wall, pretending it was his manager's head. He'd had it with their crap. Being demoted to training newbies, just because some Orinian didn't like his attitude. It was bullshit.

He took his trousers off and pulled his N-Tac suit on. What he needed now was to blast it all away. There was a Life Through Death immersion where they'd edited intense music over Delilah Dare's death, as she shot into space attached to the outside of the Hudson/Kiyoshi space elevator. That's what he wanted right now. To die over and over again. Anything to take him away from this pathetic life.

The immersion pod door clicked shut behind him and its internal fingers attached themselves to his N-Tac suit, lifting his considerable bulk into the air. Everything flashed white, and Samuel found himself floating in the center of his bubble. All around, his flickering tiles teased their immersion contents. Samuel quickly dismissed his notifications and tapped on his VNP before opening Dark Search. He searched the Life Through Death immersions, nearly flicking the latest one away in his haste to experience Delilah Dare's death. Then he saw it was a live immersion. It wasn't a recording; it was happening right now, with other people just like him. Samuel cursed himself for not knowing this was happening, not that he'd have made it home from work any earlier, nevertheless, he'd nearly missed it. Samuel tapped the tile and everything flashed white.

The white resolved into a crowd of people stood on a mountain top, overlooking a dark lake that snaked away between lush green foothills.

The crowd, however, were not looking at the lake. Their faces were cast gently upwards at the figure of Grandmaster Vonhoff, who stood on a platform the immersion program had placed in the sky.

"...and as a Lumen facilitator I had to deal with many types of people," Grandmaster Vonhoff said "and no matter who spoke, the citizens off the street searching for salvation, or the other facilitators, everyone spoke utter nonsense. They were endlessly regurgitating some thing, some nugget of wisdom they had heard somewhere, trying to make themselves appear intelligent. They were not intelligent. Idiots surrounded me."

Samuel laughed "Tell me about it."

The person next to Samuel, an older man with a bushy mustache, gave him a look and tutted. Samuel shrugged and brought his attention back to Grandmaster Vonhoff.

"What these people had missed, for years they'd trying to manifest the wrong thing. Heck, for a while even I was doing the same. You see, we've had knowledge passed down to us, knowledge from people who we believed were wise, saying that when your joy comes through the misery of others, that is wrong. And we all want to believe that. But why is it so hard then?"

A crisp air blew among those gathered. No one dare answer.

"Because it is not true. Look at the world. It is based on suffering. If joy isn't based on the suffering of others, why is suffering so prevalent?"

Grandmaster Vonhoff paused to look around the crowd. Samuel gazed upwards, watching the grandmaster's white and red robes blow gently in the wind. He loved this man. The grandmaster had helped him understand why he'd been obsessed with reliving LV creators experiences. And when he'd felt ashamed at getting sexual gratification from the death immersions of Lana Edge and Delilah Dare, Grandmaster Vonhoff had shown him he had nothing to be ashamed of. It wasn't his fault. In fact, he was gaining life through their deaths. Cleansing his soul.

Just when Samuel thought the great man would speak again, he turned and stared straight at Samuel. It was like a ray of light, straight from heaven. Samuel felt his spirit glow.

"The real question is," the grandmaster continued, casting his gaze once more across the crowd, "why are you suffering?"

A murmur rolled through the audience.

"Why are you the one slaving away creating immersions on Viribus B..."

Someone in the crowd hollered agreement.

"...or breaking your back on one of the many planets in the Demesne system..."

A section of the crowd whooped.

"...all so the Orinians can live a life of luxury?"

Booing rippled through the crowd at the mention of the Orinians. Samuel joined in. For once in his life, he felt like he could truly express himself without fear of being judged. For once in his life,

Samuel felt like he was home.

"So, what is there to do?" Grandmaster Vonhoff said, holding his arms out wide.

"Tell us," someone in the crowd shouted.

"We'll do anything," another voice called.

"Well," Grandmaster Vonhoff smiled, and it may have been a trick of the immersion, but his face appeared to grow larger. "I think we have been shown the answer already. Killer X has shown us. He's shown us what its like to experience death. He's shown us what its like to live through death. But more than that, he's shown us that those who cheapen themselves for the entertainment of others are not worthy."

"If we don't want the Orinians controlling us, then we must take action. If you want to stop your suffering, you must take action. God will not lift a finger for you. No, you must do it yourself. We must continue killer X's work!"

The crowd went wild. People hollered, people clapped, and all the time Samuel felt his spirit grow. The feeling rose in him, a wave of clarity washing away the uncertainty. For he now knew why he'd found Grandmaster Vonhoff. It was because he was the one. He was the one who had realized something that idiot Jakowski couldn't figure out. He was the one who knew who the final victim was meant to be.

"It's me! It's me!" Samuel cried out. At first no one noticed, but as he kept on screaming, people next to him turned towards him. "It's me, it's me.

I'm the one."

Finally, the crowd died down and everyone stared at Samuel.

"I'm the one grandmaster. It's me, it's me," Samuel shouted again. "I am the one who can continue what killer X started."

The crowd, now deadly silent, turned to stare at Grandmaster Vonhoff. The gentle face of the grandmaster regarded Samuel with a soft, bemused expression. Then he laughed.

"You? What are you talking about?" the grandmaster snorted. Now the entire crowd burst into riotous laughter. The surrounding people backed away and pointed and stared.

"Him?" One woman said, her face contorted in disgust. "What's he going to do? Kill the Orinians by trapping them in one of his neck folds?"

"Orinians?" Samuel said, confused. He could feel his face getting red in his immersion pod. "No. The last victim is BonnyB-GG."

The crowd stared at him with frowns on their faces.

"You know," Samuel said. "The child born on the sabbath day, is bonny and blithe, and good and gay."

The crowd was silent. Then, almost as if a conductor had flicked his baton, at once the entire crowd burst into belly slapping laughter.

A tightness closed around Samuel's chest as memories of school came flooding back. As the laughter continued, Samuel exited the immersion.

The door to his pod burst open, and Samuel stumbled out.

"Stupid idiots." The heat under his N-Tac suit became unbearable, so he stripped it off with anger. "I'll show them. They don't know. Only I know it was meant to be BonnyB-GG. Only I can finish what killer X started."

Samuel pulled his clothes and sneakers on in a rush, then grabbed some tape. He stomped out of his apartment into the corridor while pulling a strip of tape off the roll. As he approached Geraldina Monette's door, he reached out with the tape and stuck it over the door sensor. Then, in one motion, Samuel leaned his hip into Geraldina's door until the flimsy metal bent enough for the lock to pop open.

Inside, the short reception corridor was dark and quiet. The sound of an old fashion Ubiquity display playing back a 2D program came from another room. Samuel gripped the drawer in the sideboard where Geraldina had shown him her gun. He slid it open slowly to reveal the shiny gray killing instrument inside. He reached down and lifted it out of the drawer, making sure not to make any noise.

The gun felt cool in Samuel's hand and was heavier than he expected. He'd never held a gun before, let alone shot one. Private citizens weren't allowed to own them. This sudden realization made Samuel pause. What was he doing taking a gun from Cit Monette? He suddenly felt foolish, and his face flushed. Then images of the laughing crowd flooded his mind. He wasn't foolish. He was finally doing something with his life. He wasn't going to sit back anymore and let himself suffer. No. He was going to take action. He was going to finish what killer X had started. He was going to kill BonnyB-GG.

CHAPTER FOURTEEN: JAGGER JAKOWSKI

"As I said, Donny Zaytsev isn't the killer. If you'd just liste—"

"Yes, yes," Murray Murnaghan said over Jakowski. "We know. Pherson City Security is incompetent. Okay everyone, we need to break for a quick commercial but stay with us, as next up we have a guest who claims he can prove the lovable kids character, Lenny Lima, is a satanic symbol used by devil worshipers. Don't go anywhere now."

Jagger threw his glass through the newscast image that hung in front of him. Murray Murnaghan had made him look like a fool. He should have known that going on KOS News was a mistake. It was too trashy, but it was the only news channel that would take him. He'd just wanted to get the message out there. Pherson City Security had the wrong man. He could see it. Why couldn't anyone else?

Jagger stood up from the table in his apartment and thought about cleaning up the drink he'd spilled. He shook his head and instead grabbed his jacket. What he needed now was a whiskey at Le Petit Zinc. As he approached his apartment door, a call notification flashed up in his vision. Jagger sighed. It was Kameke Okonkwo. She'd been calling all day, but he'd been ignoring her. He walked back through to his living area and sat down. Better to answer the call now than in an hour when he planned to be blind drunk.

He sat facing his Ubiquity wall display and commanded the call to be answered on it. Kameke Okonkwo appeared. Her face looked tired.

"Cit Okonkwo, I—"

Kameke Okonkwo held up a hand. "Cit Jakowski, you can never know when a chicken sweats because of their feathers. But sometimes a chicken come right to you, and you pluck it and see what it really is."

Jagger sighed. "Cit Okonkwo, I—"

"It's over now. But you going on the newscasts just keep reminding me. I want resolution Cit Jakowski, I want to move on. You must let this go. Please move on. I have."

Kameke Okonkwo cut the call, leaving Jagger staring at the black Ubiquity display. He blew air out his nose and shook his head. Even Grace's mother didn't believe him. What was the point?

He stood up harshly, sending his chair tumbling to the floor behind him. Jagger stomped out of his apartment while commanding Ubiquity to order him a SkyTaxi. He thought he needed a whiskey before. He really needed it now.

#

The clack of pool balls rung out from the far end of Le Petit Zinc. Cheerful laughter from the group of men playing scratched at Jagger's irritable mood. Behind him a woman was having a loud conversation via Ubiquity, and at the end of the bar the old timer Mac was repeating one of the five stories he knew.

Lolo placed a pint of lager and a glass of whiskey in front of Jagger. She leaned on the counter and frowned.

"Why is zit, zat your are always sad?"

Jagger looked at her under his furrowed brow. "I'm not sad, I'm pissed off."

"Well," Lolo said, pushing herself off the bar, waving a hand, "Zat is okay then. He's fine, everyone. Zis man is pissed off. Nothing to worry about here."

Jagger could feel the other patrons look over at him. He hunched forward over his drinks, as if he could retreat into them.

"Hey," a voice said from behind him, "weren't you on KOS News the other night? You were ranting about a nursery rhyme or something?"

Jagger ignored the voice and took a swig of his lager.

"I don't know why you're making a fool of yourself, even if the guy who surrendered is not the killer. Who cares? Their just LV girls, whoring themselves out."

"Bod," another voice said. "Didn't you used to follow Delilah Dare?"

"Yeah, so? She died. There's always another LV

girl to replace them. I kinda got a kick off her death. It was better than most of her immersions."

Laughter came from the other voice. "You're sick bod."

"Don't you know it." The voices got closer now. "Hey, this is also the guy that threatened Judge Goode the other day. Made a right fool of himself. I recognize you man."

Jagger continued to ignore them and knocked back his whiskey.

"Hey, man. Was that you?"

Jagger felt someone slap his arm. He was off his seat before he knew what he was doing. His fist automatically launched itself at the first guy's smug face. It missed. A quick sidestep foiled Jagger and he fell after his fist, past the smug guy's torso, onto the floor by the old timer, Mac's, stool. Before he could rise, Lolo had rounded the bar and put herself between Jagger and the two men.

"It's okay guys. He's had one too many. Nothing to worry about. I'll handle him." Even though she was only small, Lolo commanded respect worthy of her character.

The two guys that had tensed up, expecting another drunken assault, relaxed. They look at each other and shook their heads. Jagger was clearly too pitiful for them to waste anymore time on. They turned and retreated to their corner of the bar.

Lolo helped Jagger back up onto his stool. Nothing had been hurt except his ego, and not for the first time this week.

"Thanks," Jagger said, looking into Lolo's eyes. "You're my hero."

Lolo snorted, then smirked, lifting her arm

and flexing her bicep. "Yes, I am zee superwoman. Defender of drunks, savior of fools."

Now it was Jagger's turn to laugh. Then a dark look fell over his face.

"Am I the only person in this city who thinks its not okay to be murdering people?"

"You know, maybe zey are right?"

"What? Not you too?"

Lolo shrugged. "I don't want people to die, but maybe you can't save everyone, Jagger Jakowski. So," Lolo placed a hand on Jagger's leg. "What's zis about you attacking Judge Goode?"

Jagger sighed and shook his head. "I never attacked her. I was trying to warn her. Everyone just got the wrong end of the stick."

"Oui, oui." Lolo raised her eyebrow, then she made her way back around to her side of the bar. "It's always everyone else that's wrong. Never you."

"In this case, it was." Jagger picked up his lager and took a large swig. "I decoded killer X's code. It's from a nursery rhyme. The last line indicated it would be Judge Goode that would be killed."

Lolo picked up a glass and dried it with a cloth. "Why didn't you go to security?"

Jagger exhaled loudly. "They're pissed off at me too. Just because I exposed that there was a killer, when security were ignoring the case." Jagger downed the last of his lager, slid off his stool, and made for the exit.

"What was zis nursery rhyme, anyway?"

Jagger stopped. "Monday's child is fair of face. Tuesday's child is full of grace. Wednesday's child is full of woe. Thursday's child has far to go. Friday's child is loving and giving. Saturday's child works hard for a living. And the child born on the sabbath day, is fair and wise and good in every way."

Jagger placed his hand on the exit to Le Petit Zinc and pushed it open to the windy, perpetual sunset of Pherson City.

"Hey," Lolo said. "Zat's not how it goes."

The wind was colder than usual, and the street was getting busy. Jagger turned back.

"What's that?"

"Ze end of the rhyme. Zats not how it goes."

Jagger stood in the wind swept doorway of Le Petit Zinc and allowed himself to feel a glimmer of hope that he might catch the killer yet.

#

Jagger's endocrine patch whirred. ClearHead and WideAwake were administered into his system as he ran down the street.

And the child born on the sabbath day, is bonny and blithe, and good and gay. How could I have been so stupid, Jagger thought? It'd not even occurred to him there might be an alternative ending to the nursery rhyme his mother had told him as a child.

Jagger dodged and twisted through the thickening crowd on his way to the nearest LZ. The streets were filling up as citizens finished work and made their way out for food and entertainment, or home to their families. Up ahead the landing zone was busy with rotocar's taking off and landing. People risked their lives ducking under the slowly descending vehicles, all to gain an extra few seconds rather than waiting for them to land. Jagger spotted a couple getting out of a

SkyTaxi and rushed over. He slid into the passenger cabin as the last person exited.

"Hey," a man said, stood at the rotocar door, "that's my taxi."

Jagger looked up at the young man. He was dressed in the latest fashion of retoweave fabrics and had a pulsing tattoo that ran down his face onto his arm. The tattoo might have worried some of the older residences of Pherson City, but it didn't concern Jagger. He knew this tattoo was purely for fashion.

"Not anymore," Jagger said with a snarl. The young man hesitated, considering his options. Jagger balled his fists. "Get outta here."

The young man stepped back, allowing Jagger to close the door. He instructed the automated SkyTaxi to take him to his apartment. As the rotocar rose into the sky, Jagger think-told Ubiquity to search through for any Live Vicariously creators with the keywords bonny, blithe, good or gay in their name. A moment later the results were displayed via his DigiLenses hanging in the passenger cabin of the SkyTaxi. Jagger cursed. There were one hundred and three of them. The first one was called Adorable Bonny. Jagger think-told Ubiquity to open her LV channel so he could read her description.

Thanks for checking out my channel. I may look adorable, but I'm anything but innocent. Check me out and you'll experience my performances with both guys and gals. I love being submissive and told what to do.

Jagger went back to the search results. The next few were in the same vein. Jagger sighed, closed the results, and looked out the SkyTaxi's dirty window. The logo of the multi-system travel company, WunderLust, twinkled and rotated in front of a skyscraper. Its edges blurred by the muck on the window.

Why am I doing this, Jagger wondered. *Security doesn't care, and all I've got from trying to help is to be made a fool on a newscast.*

The SkyTaxi swung around the building with the WunderLust projection, and in the distance Jagger saw the Ziegler Tower. Its giant Z shimmered on the side of the building. The side Grace Okonkwo, performing as Lana Edge, had fallen to her death on. That was why he was doing this. Everyone deserved justice, even if Pherson City Security didn't care.

Rain began to rattle on the roof of the SkyTaxi as Jagger brought the list that matched his search term up, and think-told Ubiquity to show him the next result. Someone called BonnyB-GG. An image of a busty, scantily clad woman appeared holding a small dog. Below her picture was a description of her Live Vicariously channel.

I'm Bonny, he's Blithe, he's good, I'm gay. On my channel you'll experience the hottest—

Jagger didn't need to read anymore. This had

to be the one. The SkyTaxi shook as it started to descend to the LZ on the roof of Jagger's apartment building. He think-told Ubiquity to show him BonnyB-GG's immersions and had a wave of panic rushed over him. The SkyTaxi landed with a thump and Jagger rushed out the barely open door. BonnyB-GG was broadcasting live, and she'd called her immersion broadcast, Taking A Break. I Need To Be Alone.

Rain lashed across Jagger's face as he dashed to the roof entrance of his building. He needed to get his gun quick. He had a feeling that in this immersion, BonnyB-GG would not be alone.

CHAPTER FIFTEEN: SAMUEL WHEATIES

Rain whipped into Samuel's face as he walked along the deserted riverbank by the old production factories. Before the Demesne system, with its rich resources, had been colonized, these factories would have been running around the clock to supply the Governance all manner of goods. Now they sat idle, their purpose stolen from them. The colossal structures loomed like mighty skeletons from another era. An era before immersion entertainment was Viribus B's largest export, an era before BonnyB-GG could have been a star.

Samuel knew exactly where BonnyB-GG would be. He'd been viewing a 2D version of her broadcast minified in his vision the whole journey over. His SkyTaxi had dropped him a few hundred meters away, in a spot obscured from BonnyB-GG by the curve of the river and a giant factory, so not to alert her of his presence.

"I'm going to do something. I'm going to be someone," Samuel said under his breath, as he waddled along as fast as his chunky legs would carry him. It was moments like this that Samuel cursed himself for not taking better care of himself. BonnyB-GG wasn't walking fast, but it was going to take a tremendous effort for him to catch up with her, especially if he didn't want her to hear him. He had to keep his pace slow enough that he wasn't panting too heavily, but fast enough to catch her.

As his heart labored to keep his large frame moving, Samuel felt the usual fingers of depression creep up over his shoulders to take a firm grip on him. Thoughts of self-loathing flash across his mind. What was he doing? He was a loser. There was a reason he did nothing with his life, why he didn't take action. He was a waste, that was why. He'd tried a few times to pull himself up and join the ranks of cheerful people, if that's what they really were, but he'd always failed. And it had usually been spectacularly embarrassing. Like when he'd asked Lindsay Bradley out in high-school and she'd rejected him. Not just rejected him but had shammed him in front of half the school for even thinking she'd be interested in someone like him.

The rain pounded Samuel vehemently. Like it knew he was a loser and was laughing at him. Samuel came to a stop and let tears mix with the rain. Who was he kidding? He couldn't do this. He couldn't actually kill her, could he? Of course, this was just another pathetic endeavor he tried, that he would fail at. Fail at before he even started.

The image of Grandmaster Vonhoff appeared in his mind, like he was viewing him through his DigiLenses. The grandmaster was laughing at him. Laughing at him for what a pathetic human being Samuel Wheaties actually was. Along with Grandmaster Vonhoff's voice, Samuel could hear the laughter of every other person who'd thought he was a loser. Lindsay Bradley's shrill, nasally cackle, his boss' low chortle, Yuval's snort of disapproval, and finally his parents sniggers at yet another failure by their pitiful son.

Samuel's chest heaved in and out in the downpour. Steam rose from his body as his usual despondency gave way to anger. *Screw those people,* thought Samuel. *Screw them and their spiteful arrogance. They don't think I can do this. But I can. I can be something. I can kill BonnyB-GG.*

Gripping Geraldina Monette's gun tighter, Samuel launched his body forward. He didn't care about making a noise now. He just wanted to kill her and prove to all the haters that he could do it.

Over the river, wind blew sheets of rain around the side of the abandoned factory building in front of him. Samuel pounded the concrete pathway, trying to gain ground on BonnyB-GG. Scraps of metal lay in his path and spots of vegetation had burst through the concrete, proving humanity's existence would soon be forgotten if it were to leave this planet.

As Samuel rounded the edge of the factory, his

heart jumped. There she was. BonnyB-GG stood directly in front of him, ten meters away. Her hands lay on the concrete wall as she gazed over the river so Samuel could view her profile. An umbrella extended out of her back, a meter above her, its wide clear plastic dome kept the Live Vicariously creator's immaculately styled brunette hair dry. Even viewing her from just her profile, Samuel could see that she was beautiful, truly beautiful. Doubt again flashed through his mind. Who was he to remove someone as beautiful as this from the world? Then anger dismissed it. Why did she get special treatment just because fate had dealt her better looks than him? She was probably standing there complaining about how hard her life was, like she had any idea. Like she had any idea what someone like him went through. Like she knew what it was like to have people look at you and turn away. Like she knew what it was like to have no one, not even your parents, believe in you. Like she knew what it was like to have to kill a person to prove that you are someone, that you're not a waste of space, that you are not a loser.

Samuel raised the gun. He gripped it in two hands out in front of him and aimed it at BonnyB-GG's head as she stared out over the gray river. As if on cue, she shook her head. Samuel frowned. Could she see him? BonnyB-GG moved her arm down to her waist, then raised it out in front of her, holding a—

Samuel gritted his teeth and pulled the trigger.

CHAPTER SIXTEEN: BONNYB-GG

BonnyB-GG walked along the riverbank, below the dark brooding buildings that matched her mood so well. She'd told her fans when she'd started broadcasting that she needed them to experience this. She needed them to experience walking in the rain, in the cold, to even get close to feeling what she felt right now. BonnyB-GG think-told Ubiquity to show her the number of users logged into her Live Vicariously immersion. Thirty thousand, three hundred and sixty-four flashed up in her vision. Of course Ubiquity wouldn't broadcast that number out. It would only broadcast what she actually saw and felt.

Thirty thousand, three hundred and sixty-four. It was a disappointing number for BonnyB-GG. It was less than half her followers and a third less than what she normally got on a live broadcast. She cursed herself for rushing the immersion title and description. She hadn't spent time, as she normally would, testing them in Ubiquity's ranking programs to see how they'd score. The news had been too upset. It didn't matter now. Here she was.

She'd picked this spot to pause, because she

knew from her morning runs it would offer the sullen type of view she wanted when looking out over the river, and the building behind her was dark and brooding.

The concrete wall felt wet and rough under her hands. She hoped this sensation translated to her users. She let her vision rest on the gray river being ravaged by the rain.

"Hey y'all, I'm sorry this isn't my usual type of immersion," she said over the sound of the rain hammering the plastic umbrella over her head. "I just... I don't know how to tell you this. I have some bad news."

BonnyB-GG watched as the number of users viewing her immersion started to fall. Instinctively she brought her hand to her body to touch herself, to give her users what they wanted, but she stopped. *They really are using me, aren't they?* The thought flashed across her mind.

Anger welled up inside BonnyB-GG now. It took all her willpower not to lash out at the remaining users. It wasn't them, after all, that had exited her immersion. Lashing out would only alienate even more of her fans. She took a deep breath to compose herself.

"It's Blithe. My beautiful little fur baby Blithe. We were heading over to the Sector 23 shopping complex, and he got away from me. I don't know what it was that he saw. Maybe a rat? But just as we approached the LZ, he sprung out of my arms and ran away. The descending rotocar wouldn't have seen him run under it. I... I—"

BonnyB-GG felt tears coming. She shook her head, reached into her pocket and pulled out a mirror so her fans could see how upset she was. In the mirror, her eyes welled up and behind her something red moved in the dark.

A loud crack, like thunder sounding a meter from her head, made BonnyB-GG scream. Two more cracks came in quick succession. BonnyB-GG dropped the mirror and sank to her feet, knocking her umbrella away as she did. It took her a moment to realize she was fine. She wasn't hurt. She twisted around so her back was to the concrete wall. In front of her, a hooded figure lay still on the rain soaked floor. Dark blood mixed with the rain and drained towards her. BonnyB-GG screamed and stood up. It was then she saw the red X lit up inside the hood. It was the killer. The killer who had murdered Harry Hard, Delilah Dare and the other Live Vicariously creators.

Someone was near to her. She screamed when she saw a large man a few meters away holding a gun. His eyes were wide. When he noticed her staring at him, he dropped the gun. BonnyB-GG ran towards the man and buried her face in his wet, squishy chest and squeezed him tight.

"Thank you," BonnyB-GG's muffled voice said. "Thank you so much. You saved my life."

"I... I..." the man's voice was shaky, "I saved your life."

Footsteps running behind them made BonnyB-GG turn. A man in a long black jacket with dark hair and a beard carrying a gun appeared. BonnyB-GG screamed again and squeezed the large man.

"Wheaties, calm her down," the man with the long black jacket said as he put his gun away and crouched by the body.

The large man called Wheaties patted BonnyB-GG on the back. "It's okay. I know him. It's Jagger Jagkooski."

"Jakowski," the man said as he stood and approached them. "What are you doing here?"

BonnyB-GG realized the man called Jakowski wasn't talking to her. He was addressing Wheaties.

"I... I..." Wheaties sounded uncertain.

"The poem?"

"Yeah. The child born on the sabbath day, is bonny and blithe—"

"—and good and gay." Jakowski said, finishing Wheaties thought. "Well, you di—"

The roar of a roto descending quickly cut Jakowski off. They all looked up, shielding their eyes from the rain being whipped towards them. A Pherson City Security roto-transport hung in the sky above them.

"Everyone, kiss the floor and put your hands behind your heads," a voice from the roto-transport boomed and a light from the undercarriage blinded them.

BonnyB-GG suddenly felt awkward. She'd been holding onto this large man, this stranger called Wheaties, for minutes now. She quickly released him and lowered herself to the floor. The two men did the same. As the roto-transport landed, wind, rain and bits of dirt flew along the floor into their faces. The roto's door slid open and the unmistakable sound of a metallic foot stomped onto concrete. An ersatz.

Then more stomping. BonnyB-GG turned her head and observed a least four humanoid machines standing by the roto-transport. Rain bounced off their dark chrome bodies. Two moved to the dead body, and the other two stomped over to where they lay on the floor.

"Jakowski?"

BonnyB-GG saw Jakowski twist his head upwards towards the ersatz.

"Yeah," he said. "Collins, is that you?"

The ersatz said nothing. Instead, it bent forwards and gripped Jakowski by the scuff of his neck and lifted him into the air.

"Hey," Jakowski said. His arms shot up to hold on to the chrome wrist, his legs flailing wildly.

"Relax," the ersatz said. "I just want a word." Jakowski's legs settled a little, but he still didn't look comfortable as the ersatz stomped off with him. About ten meters away, it lowered Jakowski to the ground, and the two started talking. Or at least Jakowski was talking. His mouth was moving, and he gesticulated frantically. The ersatz stood still in front of Jakowski. It could have been speaking, but there was no way for BonnyB-GG to tell.

After a few minutes, Jakowski went silent. He stared up at the head of the ersatz and nodded. Then he turned and walked away. BonnyB-GG watched to see if he would look back. He never did. His black jacket flapped in the wind and rain, as he traveled along the concrete path by the riverbank, away from the scene of the murder.

The ersatz that spoke with Jakowski stomped over to where BonnyB-GG and Wheaties lay on the wet floor. It signaled the other ersatz, who bent down and lifted the large man next to BonnyB-GG to his feet.

"Well, Samuel Wheaties," the first ersatz said. "It looks like you're a hero."

CHAPTER SEVENTEEN: SAMUEL WHEATIES

The rusty elevator door opened on Samuel's floor of his apartment building. He stepped out into the corridor, with a strange sensation of both tiredness and elation running through his body. His clothes were still damp. And the small confines of the elevator made him realize how much he stank. He couldn't wait to get into his apartment and take a shower. As he treaded wearily along the corridor, Geraldina Monette's door opened.

"There you are," Geraldina said. "Our hero has returned!"

"Hey, Cit Monette," Samuel said sheepishly. He tried to walk past her, but his elderly neighbor block his way. "I'm not really a hero."

Geraldina Monette shook her head and swatted the air in front of her. "Of course you are. All the newscasts are saying so."

"Really?"

"Yes. You're being praised for helping Pherson City Security. And that one interview you did has been on repeat almost non stop."

Samuel smiled. After security had arrived, they'd spoken with Jakowski, and for some reason he'd left. When they took Samuel to the security station. They'd said, as far as security was concerned, Jakowski had nothing to do with this. It was all his actions. To be honest, the whole thing was all a bit of a blur. It had happened so fast. He'd aimed the gun, fired that first shot. Then he must have fired the other two shots, but that part was hazy. The next thing he knew, BonnyB-GG was hugging him tight. Pherson City Security said they could charge him for carrying an illegal weapon, but since he had helped catch killer X, they would let it slide.

When he left the security station, Samuel had been shocked to see hundreds of people waiting for him. They were all chanting his name, calling him a hero. A newscast crew from VB News had been there to capture an interview with him on the steps of the security station. At first he'd been shy of the recorders. He looked like a mess, but as the crowd kept on chanting his name, and the news anchor clearly didn't care what he looked like, he'd stopped and talked.

It was a strange sensation. After years of people ignoring you on the street, after years of no one caring what you said, to have a news crew, with its recorder, bright lights and enthusiastic news anchor in your face, it was... electrifying. The damp fatigue he'd felt simply vanished. He'd answered the questions as best as he could, though now he couldn't even remember what they had asked him. All he could remember was the chanting of the crowd. Of his name being shouted, of the love being sent his way.

Now he was back at his apartment. Some of the euphoria was fading. The multiple notifications flashing up in his vision from newscasts wanting interviews had seemed like a burden. But now he'd seen how happy Geraldina Monette was, he felt lifted again. All he needed was a hot shower and some food, and he'd be ready to speak to whoever wanted him.

Samuel was about to thank Geraldina Monette for her kind words when the elevator door creaked open again. Yuval stepped out with a dark look on his face. His hair and clothes were disheveled, and he had dried blood on his lip.

"Yuval," Samuel said. "What happened?"

Yuval stomped to his door. "Why don't you ask that old cow what happened?"

Samuel looked down at Geraldina Monette. The old lady's wrinkled face gave a dismissive gesture.

"When I found my apartment was broken into and my gun stolen, I called security," Geraldina said with a shrug.

"You didn't just call security," Yuval snapped. "You called them and said that I had stolen the gun!"

"Well, you could have."

Yuval's face distorted, making him look like a wild beast. He stormed toward Geraldina Monette. Samuel put his large frame between Yuval and the old lady.

Yuval snapped his gaze up at Samuel and halted. He shook his head and walked back to his apartment door and opened it.

"Do you have any idea what they did to me!" Yuval said, spit flying from his mouth.

Geraldina Monette shrugged. "Probably nothing you didn't deserve."

"Argh!" Yuval retreated into his apartment and slammed the door shut.

Samuel let Yuval's energy fade from the corridor before turning to Geraldina Monette. "Sorry I took your gun," Samuel said, feeling his shoulders sag a little.

Geraldina Monette looked up at him with a smile on her face. "It's fine. I'm glad you used it to stop the killer."

Samuel nodded and moved along the corridor towards his apartment. He stopped at his door and turned back.

"Why are you always so harsh on Yuval? He did nothing wrong."

"It doesn't matter," Geraldina said, a mischievous twinkle in her eye. "He could have. I know his type."

Samuel nodded and opened his door.

"Don't worry about him," Geraldina said. "Remember. You're the hero Samuel. You're the real hero."

Samuel nodded at Geraldina Monette again and closed his apartment door. Inside, he rested his large frame on the wall and smiled. He was a hero. For the first time in his life he wasn't the loser, he was the hero, and it felt good.

CHAPTER EIGHTEEN: JAGGER JAKOWSKI

"It's here," Lolo said, placing a pint of lager and a whiskey in front of Jagger.

Le Petit Zinc was quiet, with just a few customers tucked away in the corners. Jagger was thankful. He couldn't handle a loud crowd right now, but also didn't want to be alone in his apartment. He picked up the lager and took a large swig of the golden liquid. Delicious. Placing the pint glass back down, a satisfying burp rolled up his esophagus and exited his mouth.

Lolo laughed. "You seem happier now. I saw zat someone had stopped ze killer. Anything to do with you?"

Jagger knocked back his whiskey and smiled. "I'm sworn to secrecy."

"Oh, come on," Lolo said, raising her eyebrows. "Anyone one can see zat Samuel Wheaties couldn't have done what zey said he did."

"Well, I'm not supposed to say anything," Jagger said, turning the empty whiskey tumbler around in his hand. "But maybe I can be persuaded?"

A smile spread across Lolo's face. "Okay. One." She took the empty tumbler from him, moved to the back of the bar, and picked up a bottle of whiskey.

"Ahem," Jagger said, clearing his throat. When Lolo looked over, Jagger pointed to the top shelf with his eyes.

Lolo held his look, then signed. She placed the bottle she held back down, then reached up to the top shelf for the higher quality liquor.

"Okay, here is your bribe," Lolo said, placing the fresh whiskey in front of him. "Now, spill ze beans."

Jagger picked up the drink and held it to his nose. The woody, almost sweet smell made him decide to sip this whiskey instead of downing it.

"It was you."

"Moi?"

"Yes. Once I realized there was an alternative ending to the Monday's Child poem, it was easy to find out who the killer was going to target next. Wheaties had also figured it out."

Lolo raised an eyebrow. "So, he did stop the killer?"

"No." Jagger smiled and took another sip of whiskey. "I approached BonnyB-GG through one of the buildings. After what happened with Judge Goode, I didn't want to blow my cover without knowing the killer was actually there. I watched her walking along the riverside path and paused to look out over the water. What I didn't realize was killer X had hid in the same building but on the ground floor. That was, until I saw Wheaties appear out of nowhere. He must have seen the killer because he fired. His shot missed. He was lucky not to hit BonnyB-GG." Jagger shook his head and finished the whiskey. "The shot must have confused killer X, as he paused two meters from BonnyB-GG.

It was enough time for me to fire two rounds into his chest."

Jagger's eyes fell downcast.

Lolo placed a hand on Jagger's. "You did ze right thing."

"I know."

"So, why is zis Samuel Wheaties getting all the credit?"

"Ah," Jagger said, glancing up, shaking his head. "Collins thought that Captain Rafi wouldn't be too happy to hear that it was me that stopped the killer."

"But some random vigilante is okay?"

"I don't think you understand how much Captain Rafi hates my, story breaking, showing Pherson City Security up, newscast appearing, ass. The city thinks I'm a fool, remember?"

Lolo smiled. She took his empty tumbler and poured Jagger another high-quality whiskey.

"It doesn't matter zat the city thinks you're a fool. What's important is you saved zat girl. And you stopped any others from being killed."

Jagger smiled and took a sip of his whiskey.

"So," Lolo said, as she chopped up some limes. "Who was ze killer, anyway?"

"It was some guy called Radulf Berkowitz. A city facilities maintenance associate, who was angry at not making it as a Live Vicariously creator himself. He also grew up in poverty and was part of several anti-Governance grou—" A call notification flashed up in Jagger's vision.

Lolo looked up from chopping limes. "What is it?"

"I've got a call coming in."

"Good news?"

"Resolution."

Jagger accepted the video call, though he could only respond with audio as he wasn't near a Ubiquity recorder. Kameke Okonkwo's tear streamed face appeared, floating over the bar.

"Jagger Jakowski, you too much. You too much. Thank you."

Dear Reader,

Thank you for reading Live Vicariously. I hope you enjoyed reading it as much as I enjoyed writing it. I've included 4 chapters of **Residuum Offerings: Voracious Universe Book One** below for you to sample.

But before you go on to that, I'd be grateful if you left a review for Die Vicariously on Amazon, and signed up for my awesome newsletter:

ricraewrites.com/newsletter

Yours,

Ric Rae

(now read on to enjoy Residuum Offerings)

RESIDUUM OFFERINGS

VORACIOUS UNIVERSE BOOK ONE

RIC RAE

PROLOGUE: LAVESH DEKEL

A shape moved in the dark as Lavesh Dekel made his way through the crowded tables. The pounding music faded. He paused and with everyone else, turned his attention to the stage. The scene, lit from behind by a brilliant light, revealed the silhouette of a woman. Conversation in the crowd drifted away. For one, two, three heartbeats, the place froze. All eyes on the silhouetted black figure.

With the tension in the room at breaking point, intricate gold lines grew out from the silhouetted woman's navel. Thin lace spread over her body, revealing a curvaceous figure. When the gold reached her fingertips, neon pink pulsed through the lines and the woman's hip ground out a circle as the music dropped. Dekel stood with his jaw open, mesmerized and more than a little aroused. *She's stunning.* He'd never seen a woman like that before. Hell, he'd never been in a club before. Never had enough credits, in fact, he still didn't.

Remembering his reason for being at the club, Dekel pulled his eyes from the dancer, and continued to push his way through the crowd who were going wild with the pumping music. Dekel looked around at the patrons. Most were at the rougher end of average, even for citizens of Deula City. No one took notice of him though, they were either too caught up in each other or the woman gyrating on stage. She had a hunger for credits and the audience didn't let her down.

Bocco Kangra's booth sat elevated at the back of the club. Dekel's hands felt clammy so he wiped them on his trousers. He'd never met Kangra. Of course he'd seen the owner of Xenoog Industries give speeches on newscasts or in immersion, but never in real life.

Through the crowd, Dekel got his first glimpse of the notorious man. Bocco Kangra sat in a leather booth with a grin on his face. His greedy eyes watching the woman on stage. Dekel wondered if the club owner looked at all of his dancers like that.

As Dekel approached the booth, two men stepped in his way. Dekel wasn't a large man, so was used to being the short one, but these guys dwarfed him. Their heads resembled granite cubes, tons of right angles and no soft edges, and their chests and arms were bursting with muscle. How much food, or drugs, would you have to eat to get that big? *More than my weekly credits could afford*, Dekel thought.

The two goons were flaunting their bionic hands. Making a show of them to him, flexing the metal fingers, then making a solid fist that could crush his skull. Dekel noticed the right hands, their gun shooting hands, were still human however.

"Let him through," a gruff voice said from behind the two goons. They stepped aside while keeping their deep-set eyes on him.

Dekel now had his first proper look at Bocco Kangra. Initially he noticed the man's head. It was colossal. And he looked just as menacing as he did in immersion. His dark tan skin looked as tough as leather, and green eyes like a snake searching for a rat to eat. Dekel slid into the circular booth and sat opposite Bocco. The big man's piercing gaze made him uncomfortable, so he averted his and stared at the table in front of him.

"Not so cocky now, are you?" Bocco said.

Dekel felt his cheeks flush. He brought his chin further to his chest. Bocco snickered, then signaled for a waitress to come over.

A scantily clad woman appeared at the booth. "Yes, Cit Kangra?" she said over the music.

"Get me a beer and a single malt," Bocco said, his voice a deep rumble. "Tell Jimmy I want the Li-Sedol black label."

The waitress nodded and turned to Dekel, who smiled expectantly.

"He don't want nothing," Bocco said, staring at Dekel. The waitress paused for a moment. Bocco slowly turned his colossal head towards the young woman.

The waitress nodded again and left the table. Bocco returned his stare back to Dekel, who shifted in his seat.

"Cit Kangra, I can expl—"

"You don't speak." Bocco slapped his hand on the table, making Dekel jump. "You caused me a lot of bother this week. Production dropped and I have Cassius's family to handle. And all over a woman. Do you think you're some kind of hard man?"

Lavesh Dekel swallowed. His large brown eyes grew wide with fear.

"I asked you a goddamn question," Bocco said.

"Oh, I," Dekel said, stumbling over his words. "I didn't think, I mean, n—"

"You're damn right you didn't think. I'm a good worker short and half a day's production behind. Do you have any idea how hard that's going to be to make up?"

Dekel shook his head. "No. I—"

Bocco slapped his hand on the table again. "I'm speaking."

Dekel didn't breathe. He didn't dare. No matter what he said, it seemed to infuriate Bocco. Now the big man wasn't speaking. He just stared at Dekel with his piercing green eyes. Dekel couldn't stand it. The silence over the pounding music was awful, but he resisted the urge to fill the space with mindless babble.

"You're handsome, Lavesh Dekel, but it won't last," Bocco grumbled. "Especially if you keep running your mouth like you did this week."

The waitress arrived with Bocco's drinks, allowing Dekel a chance to regain his composure. The big man picked up the whiskey and held it to the light, before bringing it to his nose for a sniff.

"They only sell this to the elite in the capital city of the Governance. It's not even sold in other cities on Elyssia, just in Li-Sedol. It's the finest whiskey in all three systems." Bocco knocked back the whiskey in one gulp. He fixed Dekel with a frown. "And here I am drinking it. Do you know what that makes me?"

Confusion shot across Dekel's face, but he kept his mouth shut.

Bocco grinned. "It makes me a big-goddamn-deal. That's what it makes me. And you," Bocco jabbed a finger towards the young man. "You are screwing up my crap right now. So, what are you going to do about it, Lavesh Dekel?"

Dekel felt the blood drain from his face. He thought he might pass out for a moment, but pulled himself together. He sat up straighter in the booth.

"Cit Kangra," Dekel said. "I'm very sorry to have caused you problems. Honestly, I'll do anything to make amends. Anything you ask."

"Damn right you will," Bocco said, a smirk replacing his frown. From inside his jacket, Bocco pulled out a handgun and set it on the table between him and Dekel. "Do you know who Hari Bhat is?"

Dekel's eyes flickered between the gun and Bocco. "Hari Bhat? You mean the Lumen scholar?" Dekel knew of Bhat, as most workers in the Demesne system were. A chemical accident in a factory had badly injured the scholar as a youth. It left his skin so tender that he spent his days lying in a vat of special liquid that cooled and soothed his constantly burning flesh. Most others would have given up and died, but not Hari Bhat. From his vat of liquid, he gave rousing speeches in immersion, championing workers' rights and daring to criticize the Governance.

"Scholar?" Bocco laughed. "Bhat is no scholar. He's a troublemaker is what he is. The Governance don't want his type around."

Dekel frowned. "Since when did you care what the Governance want?"

Bocco eye's widened for a second before he slammed his fist on the table. "I care when Hari Bhat's ramblings brings their attention down on my operation." Bocco grabbed the gun off the table and pointed it at Dekel. The young man put his hands up. His face pulled back in a grimace.

"Now," Bocco continued, "I want you t—"

An odd look fell across Bocco's face. Dekel didn't know what had happened. His heart pounded. He didn't want to die. Not over that stupid fight with Cassius.

Bocco glanced at his left hand, which rested on the tabletop. His jaw dropped open. Dekel glanced down at the big man's hand. His chubby fingers and thumb, clad with gold rings, looked fine to him.

Bocco lifted his left hand up and stared at it.

"What the fuc—"

The big man screwed up his face as if he had seen something disgusting. Dekel felt his heart pound harder. Had his boss gone mad?

Bocco suddenly jerked his head back. Before Dekel realized his intentions, Bocco fired two shots into his own hand.

The two goons turned around, pulling their guns out. Bocco stared up at them, his green eyes wild. The two goons pointed their guns at Dekel, who froze with fear.

Bocco fired two shots, taking both goons out. Their bodies dropped to the floor with a loud thud. People in the club started screaming. To Dekel, the sound appeared distant, as though he were in a glass bottle while the mayhem occurred around him.

The big man opposite still had his bloody left hand raised. He dropped it. His large brows creased together in a frown of confusion and realization, then his face went pale.

Dekel's mind told him to move, to run, but he couldn't. His muscles locked with too much adrenaline. He watched as Bocco Kangra looked down at his chest.

The big man opened his mouth. "What the fu—"

Bocco turned the gun towards his chest and fired.

Hot blood splattered Lavesh Dekel's face. Booco Kangra's body slumped to the side. For a moment everything became quiet. The air was still, Dekel didn't move. Then he took a breath and reality came crashing in.

CHAPTER ONE: JAGGER JAKOWSKI

You give someone a shard of power and they think they're God. Jagger Jakowski threw a look over his shoulder at the two corporate officers hitting on some local girls, then turned back to his beer. Privileged. Young males from the Orini system always were. He'd bet a hundred credits they'd blinked in on a freight ship, here to transport back what little resources Viribus B still had to offer.

Jagger downed his beer and made to move off his stool when Lolo, the owner of Le Petit Zinc, appeared in front of him.

"Another?" she said in her French accent. Even though English was the official language of Viribus B, Pherson City still had pockets of culture and language from Old Earth, unlike the Orinian's who were homogenized.

Jagger considered Lolo's offer. "No more beer, whiskey. Straight up."

Lolo eyed him from a moment. "You want ze good stuff?"

Jagger considered how many beers he'd had and shook his head. "Bottom shelf is fine."

The small but evenly proportioned owner of the bar moved off to fetch Jagger's drink. He remembered when there might have been something between them. Jagger shook his head. Ruminating on their history was pointless, and besides, Lolo's current relationship, over a year old now, appeared to be blooming. He felt genuine happiness for her, but couldn't shake that feeling of regret from rising in his chest. *Maybe another drink is a stupid idea,* he thought.

A loud clack of pool balls behind him made Jagger tense. Just for a moment. He wondered if that reaction would ever surrender its grip on him. War's memory held long in the body. He swung around on his bar stool to where the noise originated. A bunch of Pherson City locals were crowded around a pool table, talking and laughing. He envied their age. Not that he saw himself as old. Hell, thirty-five was good age. But he couldn't help the twang of jealousy that sprang up watching the easy gaiety of the group, especially considering how he'd spent his early twenties. He'd fostered good friendships in the military, but the memories were overshadowed with pain. Jagger pushed the feelings away. He began to turn back to the bar when he noticed the two Orinian ship officers had moved the girls, one blond with head-to-toe neon tattoos, the other with bright pink hair and an interesting body mod, to a circular booth in a darker corner of the bar. He tried to make out the girl's expressions through the dim light. Both sat in the middle, with an Orinian ether side of them. They had nowhere to go.

"Hey," Lolo said from behind him. "It's here."

Jagger turned back to the bar.

"Thanks." He picked up the receipt stick next to his drink and stared at the code. His DigiLenses scanned it and the price appeared floating next to the receipt. He think-told Ubiquity to pay via the uLink node at the top of his neck and its connection to the Ubiquity network.

"Don't worry about them," Lolo said, moving along the bar picking up empty glasses and rubbish customers had left. "They know what they're doing. Deb-deb, the tattooed one, she knows how to play the rich Orinians for a drink and a meal. Maryam is more timid, but Deb-deb looks after her."

One girl laughed loudly behind him, so he guessed Lolo must be right.

"You working a tough one?"

Jagger clenched his jaw. "Just finished. A woman from Quincay, rich. Wondered what her husband was up to when he went into immersion. Said he'd been unusually happy the last month."

"That's a crime?" Lolo said as she sliced a lime and tossed the wedges into a tub.

A small smile crept up the sides of Jagger's eyes. "Actually, she had good intentions. She thought her husband paid for sex in the immersion, either from a virtual girl or a real one via an ersatz. Either way, she wanted to figure out the kink he liked so she could do it for him."

"And could she?"

The smile dropped from Jaggers face. "Not unless she regressed back past puberty."

"Quel Salaud," Lolo said, shaking her head.

"That's what she thought. Anyway, once I found out what he did with those girls, I couldn't stop until I'd located where the immersions were recorded and got security to shut it down." Jagger picked at the paper beer mat under his drink. In truth, he hadn't got security to shut it down, they didn't care. So he'd done it himself. *How much of life is saving the girl,* he wondered.

Lolo washed her knife and dried it with a cloth. "Where was it?"

"Out by the hot edge," Jagger said, referring to the area of Viribus B locked to the sun. "In one of old mining towns. Quite the immersion studio they had set up out there."

Lolo shook her head again and crinkled her face in disgust. A customer at the end of the bar called for her and she moved away, probably happy to be free of the conversation she didn't know she had got herself into.

Jagger picked up his whiskey from the silver colored bar. He felt the weight and coolness of the glass. With his eyes closed, he brought it to his face. The woody smell filled his nose. He took a sip and let it sit on his tongue before feeling the heat and vapor as he swallowed. It wasn't top shelf, but he still liked to experience that first taste as if he were a virgin.

An advert on the display above the bar broke his peaceful moment.

"We move to stay alive," the silky voice of the advert said. Shots of cheerful people traversing a beautiful green wilderness played on the display. "But we're alive to move. Take the leap past the everyday and accept the call of adventure. Let nature inspire you, let nature move you. Explore Elyssia, home of the Governance. Jump ships blink out twice a week. Scan the code for WunderLust options in your area."

Jagger snorted. As if anyone in this bar could afford a vacation to the Orini system. Hell, the majority of people on Viribus B didn't know what a vacation was. He guessed they could just dream.

"You'll never catch me going on one of those, it's witchcraft," Mack, an old timer at the end of the bar said. Jagger had shared many a late night conversation with him.

"Jump ships give you the creeps, eh?" Jagger said, waving for Lolo to get Mack a drink.

"It's not natural. Blinking out of existence like that and appearing somewhere else as if nothing happened." The old timer nodded thanks for the beer Lolo had set in front of him. "It's dealing with things we don't understand. Creatures that are dangerous."

Jagger frowned. He didn't know how the

Wilcox jump drives worked, but then again he didn't know how his connection to Ubiquity worked, beyond the basic principles. What did it matter? Multitudes of people believed in mumbo jumbo because they didn't have a technical understanding of things.

"You don't believe me, eh?" Mack said, moving a stool closer. Jagger waved for Lolo to refill his whiskey. "That's how they move the jump ship. The creatures. They ask them to move the ship."

Jagger had a vision of the long jump ship, sitting in space with hundreds of smaller ships docked to it, being grabbed by a giant gnarly claw, and pulled through a rip in reality.

"Is that right?" Jagger said, wondering how many beers the old timer had sunk. Lolo set a fresh whiskey in front of him. Her face hardened as she gazed passed her patrons at the bar.

"Oh, merde," Lolo said. "Maybe they don't know what they're doing."

A yell from the booth in the corner caught Jagger's ear. He sank his whiskey, gingerly got off the stool and turned around. The two Orinian ship officers were standing with their arms around the girls' waists, trying to get them to leave. Jagger sized up the officers. Both were in their mid-twenties, a good five years older than the girls, he reckoned. One light-skinned, with blond cropped hair, the other dark-skinned with a tight afro. Bugles in their uniforms showed good upper body physique, and they were approaching two meters tall. Jagger narrowed his eyes. He stretched out his right hand hearing a few clicks, then balled it into a fist. They had a couple of inches and maybe ten years on him. But they were Orinians. Soft. He moved towards them.

"Get off me," Deb-deb said and pushed the blond officer's arm from around her. She wore a style most girls her age on Viribus B wore. A tight crop top t-shirt and short skirt that showed swathes of neon tattooed skin.

"We gotta get a rush on Sheridan, keep hold of her," the dark-skinned officer said to his shipmate. He himself had a good grip around Maryam's waist. The girl frozen with fear.

"Shut up, Dangote," Sheridan said. He snarled at Deb-deb and clutched her arm. "Come on, girl. We're notch compared to your local trash. We can afford the best hotels in this shit-hole city."

A tall, but far too skinny local youth, stepped up to the group before Jagger arrived. "You'd better leave them alone," he said. His voice a few octaves too high to be threatening. The clink of glasses and murmuring chatter of the bar fell silent.

"Yeah, we're alright bro." The two officers gave the local guy a comical look and carried on dragging the girls towards the exit.

"Hey, I said leave them alone," the skinny youth tried again.

"Stop," Deb-deb said. She pulled herself away from Sheridan, who reached out and grabbed at her. His hand caught the top of her t-shirt, ripping it open. Deb-deb hurried her hands to cover her exposed neon breasts.

Sheridan's face lit up. "Oh hell yeah, we're definitely having fun tonight." He reached out to grab her again.

Jagger had seen enough. Luckily for the officers, his guns were locked up in his apartment. Jagger stomped passed the brave skinny youth and overhand punched Sheridan in the face. The officer's head snapped back, and he dropped to the floor. Jagger winced at the sting of skin scrapped from his knuckles. He ducked and stepped back, expecting a punch from Dangote, but nothing came. The dark-skinned officer stood rigid, his face a perfect picture of shock. Jagger took delight in handing these privileged pricks something they don't normally get. Denial.

After a second of shock, the two girls nodded to Jagger. Maryam helped Deb-deb cover herself and they ran out the door.

Sheridan, still decked out, tried to get up, but his legs wobbled and he fell back on his butt. Multicolored lights from the bar ceiling danced across his face. His shipmate reached downward and yanked him to standing. Sheridan held a hand to his bloody face. It had swelled up nicely.

They both gaped at him.

"What the hell'd you punch me for, asshole?" Sheridan spat out, trying to mask the fear on his face.

Dangote pulled some strength from his

friend's statement. His chest swelled, and he clenched his fists. Jagger knew these two clowns couldn't fight. They were just looking for easy prey. And that, he certainly was not.

Dangote found his voice. "Yeah, what you d-"

In a flash, Jagger cleared the space between them and grabbed Dangote by the collars. Jagger got right up close. Terror washed over the young man's face. The thin veneer of confidence faded rapidly and his eyes widened with the shock of being manhandled.

"Why don't you jerks go back to your ship and stay away from young girls?"

Jagger dragged the ship officer through the exit of Le Petit Zinc and threw him to the pavement. The street, busy with people out dinning or drinking, held their jackets shut to the constant winds of Viribus B. Dangote stared up at Jagger blinking rapidly, a piece of paper blowing along the street caught on his face. He pulled it off and tried to rise, but Jagger pushed him back downward with the sole of his boot.

Yellow light flooded the windy street as the door opened behind them. Jagger glanced back. Sheridan made a run at him. Jagger swivelled, grabbed the man's extended arm, meant for his face, and used Sheridan's momentum to toss him on top of his shipmate. People walking by recoiled and stared at the scene with open mouths and whispered comments.

The sound of metal stomping on concrete made Jagger turn. A security ersatz headed towards them. Pinks and blues from the nearby store lights reflected on its metallic humanoid body, giving it a strangely beautiful, but terrifying look. As it approached, Jagger read the ID number along machine's chest.

"Hey Collins," Jagger said, referring to the person who controlled this ersatz from an immersion pod in the security station.

"It's Farland. Collins' shift finished an hour ago," the security ersatz said to Jagger, then glanced at the two ship officers on the floor. "What's going on here?"

Jagger nodded to the pavement. "These two thought their authority extended further than it does. Tried to force a couple of girls to go with them. So, I showed them that's not how things go in Pherson City."

"That true?" Farland said to the ship officers.

Dangote and Sheridan helped each other up, keeping the security ersatz between them and Jagger. "We were with some girls. Having some fun. No big deal. Then this psycho comes out of nowhere and attacks me." Sheridan did his best to look small and innocent.

"Bullshit," Jagger said. "These jerks think they can just blink in to Viribus B and grab whatever they want. I'm sick of it."

"Where are the girls? Can they vouch for you?" Farland said.

Jagger screwed his lips up and sighed. "They didn't stick around once I stepped in."

Farland turned to the two officers. "Which ship you from?"

Dangote grinned. "We're third officers on the Abersychan. Blinked in yesterday,"

Shit. Jagger knew of the Abersychan. It wasn't a Governance military ship, but it might as well be. The Abersychan was a cargo ship of the Governance contractor Kolff-Ogogic. Jagger sighed and shook his head. Kolff-Ogogic specialized in immersion technologies, N-Tac suits, immersion pods and ersatz bodies. One of their major contacts was providing the ersatz's for Pherson City security.

The security ersatz turned its metallic body to Jagger and stepped closer.

"Oh, come on, Farland. You know these guys are creeps," Jagger said, holding his hands up.

"Doesn't matter. You assaulted Kolff-Ogogic officers. I've gotta take you in." Farland took a security binding from a compartment on the ersatz's leg and motioned for Jagger to turn. "Let's make this easy, shall we?"

Jagger rolled his eyes in comical disbelief to the visual recorders on the head of the metallic security avatar, then complied with its request.

"Yeah," Sheridan said, suddenly full of himself. "You hit the wrong person, asshole. You're gonna get a beating i-"

The metallic ersatz cut him off by pivoting

and striding towards him. "I suggest you two get back to your ship. Now!" The large remotely operated machine loomed above them. It could kill them with its hands, it wouldn't even need to use the arsenal of weapons it had hidden inside it. "I've noted your profiles. I don't want to catch you around any of the locals' bars. Stick to the spaceport."

The two officers didn't need telling twice. They scampered up the street as fast as the busy crowd would let them.

Yellow light flooded the street again as Lolo opened the door of Le Petit Zinc and hurled abuse at the security ersatz. Farland ignored her and continued to secure the binding. Once happy, the ersatz gripped Jagger's upper arm and moved.

Jagger shook his head and laughed as it led him away. He gazed up at the mauves of the perpetually setting sun, which lit the habitable band of Viribus B. It was beautiful, really. He made a note to gaze up more often.

Behind him he heard Lolo calling out, "Va te faire foutre, Farland!"

CHAPTER TWO: UMA ODIA

Prime Coordinator Uma Odia stood by the twenty-meter-long floor to ceiling window in her office, on planet Elyssia in the Orini system. The Governance Central Office was situated by the outskirts of Li-Sedol, capital city of Elyssia. The lavish building sat at the center of a grand garden modeled after Versailles. Views from the window on the fourth floor of the GCO, looked out over immaculately tended shrubs and fountains onto a vast lake that ran away to the Rizal mountains in the distance.

Two the left, the tall white marble buildings of Li-Sedol glimmered in the sunlight among spots of lush greens and pinks of the city's flora. Uma watched as donut shaped pods climbed the silver threads of space elevators that stretched into infinity. Each one brought down countless residuum from their space tenements to lubricate the workings of the city. Between each silver thread, lines of flying vehicles dissected the sky, taking the aristocracy gently to their destinations. While beneath the city, underground maglevs took the workers to their jobs. Leaving the ground level of Li-Sedol perfectly free for those of the elite who wished to wander and muse over the delights of life.

"There is one more item," General Hixson said. "Unfortunately, there have been a number of N-Tac deaths on Viribus B."

Uma turned from the window and raised an eyebrow. "More of our allies?"

"No. Unlike the deaths in the Demesne system, the deaths on Viribus B are from the working classes. Kolff-Ogogic say the deaths are malfunctions."

"Why are you telling me this, General?" Uma moved to her walnut desk and sat down.

"We are not sure if it is related but there has been growing unrest on Viribus B. A Lumen facilitator stirring up anti-Governance sentiment disappeared six months ago, around the same time the N-Tac malfunctions started. We're worried he'll start an uprising."

"Viribus B, break away? They'd be idiots," Uma snorted. "They're a one planet system. History aside, don't they realize the Governance doesn't need them?" Uma knew this wasn't true. Without the Egosh produced on Viribus B the Governance would be crippled. But the average Viribian didn't know this.

The general pulled his aging face into a

frown. "I'm afraid that common sense gets overridden by the righteousness of the supposed wronged."

Uma laughed at General Hixson's choice of words. "What are we doing about this?"

"I have sent in a clandestine team. Due to our worries around Viribus B's security, we've instructed them to keep a low profile and use local, non-security help, where possible."

"Good. I look forward to your report. Is that it?"

"No, prime coordinator. I have news from Sodality Member Van Basten." The general shifted in his chair. Uma knew he didn't care for the man. "All personnel have been moved over and the new facility is up and running. It should increase the number of Wilcox jumps by thirty percent a year."

"Excellent," she said. "Boothroyd and I will inspect the facility this week. Is there anything else?"

General Hixson stood, straightened his uniform and gave Uma a nod. "That is all prime coordinator." He turned and exited the office.

Uma Odia swung her chair around so she faced the floor to ceiling window looking out at the splendor of Li-Sedol. A row of birds flew across the perfectly blue sky. Anti-Governance feelings were high in the Demesne system and now on Viribus B. She would have to take action.

#

Uma Odia's face lit up as she lent on the railing and admired the rows of incubators below them. Strips of lights far above reflected on the glass pods. Stored inside were little treasures. Each one gave the Governance strength and reach. The new facility was perfect. She glanced at Operations Coordinator Livingstone Boothroyd and wondered what he was thinking. Below, technicians were busy tending to the needs of the incubation pods.

"You know," she said, motioning to the technicians. "With their face masks and white coats, they all look the same."

Her pudgy faced colleague turned with a puzzled look. He opened his mouth to say something but closed it again.

Uma laughed and slapped Boothroyd on the chest with the back of her hand. As prime coordinator, she was likely the only person in the galaxy who could slap Boothroyd without repercussions, with the exception of his wife. "A joke, Livingstone. Now, come on. What do you have to tell me about Carmine?" Uma pushed off the railing and walked alongside it.

Boothroyd scuttled beside her. The barrel shaped man had rosy skin and an air of contempt for anything other than the status quo. The status quo he and Uma had created. Uma Odia herself was the opposite of him in appearance. Where he had width, she had slender, where he kept his hair short and blond, she kept hers long and silky black, where his skin appeared pink and soft, hers radiated golden brown with a tightness that didn't betray her forty-seven years.

"Yes, well," Boothroyd said, clearing his throat. "Intelligence report's nothing unusual. He's popular with the Demesnech, he champions their voice, but other than that, he's running the system just fine."

They walked along in silence.

Carmine Pirozzi had been her pick for Demesne System Coordinator, and by all means he appeared to do a good job. After the Dissidence War she could hardly expect the Demesnech to worship her, but... something about the ambitious young man grew tension up her spine. Maybe he just reminded her too much of herself?

"These deaths in Demesne. You don't think they're related?"

"Well," Boothroyd said. "The Demesne deaths were accidents."

"Even Bocco?"

Boothroyd hesitated. "Erm, well, no. Bocco lost his mind."

"Poison?"

"His blood came back clean. Security found nothing suspicious, but these men were gangsters, so I wouldn't rule it out."

Uma stopped and turned to him. "Suspicious? They were all our men. Isn't that suspicious enough?"

"Well, that's true, but they didn't know that.

And besides, we always have others waiting to fill their shoes. Even now we're making sure the right people fill the vacuums."

"And Carmine isn't trying to place people loyal to him in?"

"It doesn't appear so."

Uma nodded. Their steps echoed out along the walkway.

"Hesse is still kicking up a fuss," Boothroyd said. "Kolff-Ogogic maintain the N-Tac deaths were malfunctions."

"Perhaps Hesse should be concerned instead why his daughter was on Viribus B in the first place."

"Quite—"

A shout from ahead cut the sentence short. The clank of metal on metal rang out. A woman's head appeared from a stairwell in front of them. At the end of the walkway, a door opened and two security personnel entered. The woman looked back and forth between the security and Odia and Boothroyd. Her face flushed and her eyes large like the two moons of Elyssia. She flung herself out of the stairwell and decided the slender woman and portly man were her best bet. She ran towards Odia and Boothroyd, barely able to keep upright in her haste.

Boothroyd made a strange sound and froze, but Uma continued walking towards the young woman. Once the woman stepped within three meters of her, Uma lifted a finger. "That's enough."

The young woman skidded to a halt. Like the rest of them, she wore white trousers and t-shirt, though she'd lost the coat and mask. She had the characteristic light build and long limbs that growing up so fast on a planet with zero-point-three standard gravity would give you. The same turned-up nose, thin lips, blond hair and blue eyes as the others. She stood panting and stared at Uma. Behind her, the two security personnel closed in. The woman glanced over her shoulder. Uma saw her considering her options.

"It's okay," Uma said and stepped gradually towards her. She looked at the security personnel and motioned for them to hold back. She liked the fact the young woman had no idea who she was.

The woman bent her frame and put her hands on her knees. Tears formed lines down her pale face. Whatever fight she'd had, it was fading.

Uma continued to approach. A warm smile lit her face, her large brown eyes projecting care unfamiliar to the young woman. Uma gambled that her instinct as a human would surrender to the idea. To the idea of love. To the idea of mother.

"It's okay, it's okay," she said again, now only a meter away. "What's wrong?"

The young technician, still bent over, gazed up at Uma. "Who am I?"

"Oh, my dear," Uma frowned and reached out a hand to her. The young woman took it and rose to full height, a half a meter taller than Uma. Even though she had a height advantage, Uma felt she could crush the woman's thin hand in hers. Having been raised on Elyssia in one-point-two standard, meant the gravity and people of this world, were weak compared to her.

"Come," she said, placing a hand on her back, guiding her to the railing. Uma felt tremors of fear in the woman's sweaty body. Below, a few technicians stopped their work and stared up at the scene. Somewhere a baby cried.

"This woman wants to know who she is," Uma Odia said out over the balcony, her voice loud and commanding. Any technicians who hadn't stopped now did and gaped upwards. "You all might want to know who you are." The tremors in the young woman's hand turned into full-blown shakes. "Well," she said, spit flying from her mouth. "Let me tell you. YOU. ARE. MINE."

With that Uma reached behind the woman's ear, like a magician about to pull a coin out. Instead, she released the concealed knife in her cuff and slit the woman's throat.

Uma watched as the blood slowly seeped from the woman's neck and cascaded to the floor. *So different in low g,* she thought. The woman fell to the ground and the security guards ran over to them.

Behind Uma, someone started clapping. She turned. Next to Boothroyd stood Sodality Member Darrison Van Basten. The man's long, thin face reminded her of the whippet dog she'd kept as a pet in childhood.

"Well done, Prime Coordinator Odia," Van Basten said. "Now I'll have to send this whole shift to be reconditioned."

Uma rolled her eyes. "If they had been better conditioned to begin with, Darrison, this wouldn't have happened."

A thin smile spread across Van Basten's face. He nodded, turned and walked away with the facility's security carrying the body of the woman following behind.

"We really need to dismantle the Sodality," Boothroyd said, once Van Basten and his security were gone. "Bring the Wilcox drive under the control of the military."

"The Sodality is part of the military," Uma said.

"Well, it doesn't act like it."

Uma smiled. "Don't worry about Van Basten. He likes to play master on this small world, but he's harmless. And we have the whole Governance, remember?"

Boothroyd snorted. "If you say so."

CHAPTER THREE: JAGGER JAKOWSKI

Lolo placed a fresh pint of lager in front of Jagger. Somewhere far off a couple talked loudly, and a man played darts. Bubbles slowly flowed to the top of the golden liquid. Jagger picked his beer off the bar and took a swig. He should've gone home after a night in security, but he needed a drink and didn't want to drink alone. Now here he sat, on a stool, drinking by himself.

His knuckles throbbed. He considered patching some NoPain, but decided he'd let the alcohol do the work. The cell hadn't been too bad. Just him and twelve drunks. Thankfully, no one had been in a fighting mood. His recent work helping catch a serial killer of Live Vicariously girls gave him some credit with Viribus security, enough for him to get a slap on the wrist. But they warned him not to push it.

Along the bar he heard his name being said. A woman with blue hair, eyebrows and lips spoke to Lolo. The owner of Le Petite Zinc looked over his way and nodded. Jagger rolled his eyes. He wasn't in the mood to start a new job. The woman made her way towards him. He wondered what it would be, cheating husband, runaway kid. Whatever it was, he wasn't interested.

"Are you really Jagger Jakowski, the immersion investigator?"

Jagger gave her a sideways look. She really did like blue. Not only did the woman have blue hair, eyebrows and lips, but she'd also had unusually deep blue eyes. He ignored her and took another swig of his beer.

The woman stared into space. Jagger recognized the look. Accessing Ubiquity. Probably checking his profile.

"Rough night?" The woman said sitting down on the stool next to him, obviously happy he was who she wanted.

"You could say that." Jagger caught a glimpse of himself in the mirror behind the liquor bottles opposite. His dark brown hair stuck up in all directions, and his stubble did nothing to hide the tiredness on his face.

The woman smiled. "I'm Elkie," she said, then turned towards Lolo. "Can I get two of whatever beer this is?" Elkie pointed to Jagger's beer.

She wasn't from Pherson City then. The local beer was the city's nickname. Plus her accent was definitely not Viribian, but he couldn't quite place it. He didn't know every local accent across all the Governance planets, but generally each system had a certain sound.

Lolo set the fresh beers in front of them. Jagger swigged his drink, waiting for the woman to start, but she seemed content to keep quiet.

Jagger broke the silence. "So, what is it then? Cheating husband or did your hair stylist do a runner?"

Elkie laughed "No need to be a dickhead." She took a gulp of her beer. "Actually, it's more serious than that."

"Oh, really?"

"Yeah."

"Well, are you going to tell me? 'cause it may not look like it, but I actually have things to do."

"Okay, one sec," Elkie said and stared into space again.

A moment later a notification flash up at the side of Jagger's vision. She'd had sent him something. Jagger sighed and think-told Ubiquity, via the uLink node at the top of his neck, to open the message. A list of names grouped into twos appeared in the space in front of his eyes.

"So, what are these, your ex-lovers?"

"Nope. They're the names of people who've died in immersion over the last six months."

Jagger turned to look at Elkie. The yellow light from the bar softly lit her face, but she looked serious.

"People don't die in immersion," he said.

"These did. N-Tac malfunctions are the official reasons."

"N-Tac malfunctions?" Jagger furrowed his brow. N-Tac's were the suits you wore to feel the sensations of the immersion you were in. The Nano-Tactile suits, to give them their full name, comprised of thousands of minute machines that worked in conjunction with each other to give a sense of pressure and heat. How accurately they represented those all depended on the amount of money you paid for a suit.

Elkie nodded. "They say the suits went wrong and crushed them."

"Jesus." Jagger shook his head. "Can't imagine that's a good way to die. But I'm guessing you don't think the suits malfunctioned?"

"I..." Elkie began and stopped. She looked at the bar, her forehead crinkling in thought. Finally, she turned to face Jagger. "Look at the list. Whenever a supposed malfunction happened, two people died. Two people in completely different places died at the same time."

Jagger checked the list again to confirm. "What do you care about a load of N-Tac malfunctions?"

"One of them was my friend."

Jagger noticed a slight change in Elkie's complexion. It might have been the bar lights, but the slight flush combined with the quick glance away, Jagger was certain she was lying.

"Okay. What d'ya want me to do about it? I find cheating spouses, runaway rich kids, you'd be better off speaking to Viribus security."

Elkie turned back to the bar and drank some of her beer. "Viribus security don't seem to care. They're happy with Kolff-Ogogic's view that the deaths are simply malfunctions and well within reasonable failure rates."

Kolff-Ogogic again. Jagger shook his head and laughed. Reasonable failure rates. Unbelievable, these corporations could literally get away with murder.

"So, what are you asking?"

Elkie turned back to him and moved closer. Her strange eyes peered into his. "I want you to investigate what's really happening."

Jagger finished his beer and called for Lolo to get him a whiskey. "Look. I'm sorry about your friend, but I find living people, not dead."

"Well, I want you to investigate the truth of what really happened in these N-Tac malfunctions, and I want to help you."

"What?"

"I want to enter immersion with you and help," Elkie said.

Jagger laughed. "Oh, no, no. Look. I don't know who you think you are, but I don't work with other people."

"This time you will. I can pay whatever you want."

"Oh, you think you can just throw money at me and I'll be your dog?" Jagger said in a voice that brought looks from around the bar. He was sick of rich out of systemers. Coming to Viribus B thinking they could do what they liked, as long as they had money.

Lolo appeared with his whiskey. "Everything okay?"

Jagger picked up the whiskey and downed it. "Everything's just fine. This woman here was just leaving. Actually, no. I'll make it easier." Jagger got off his stool. "I'm leaving."

"Hey, dickhead," Elkie called after him.

Jagger pushed his way through the door and stepped out into the windy mauve night. There were countless bars in Pherson city, where people wouldn't treat him like crap.

#

Jagger snapped awake with the faces of Aisling, Dursun and Phife screaming in pain, still in his mind. He shook away the dream of his old attack team. With his mouth drier than the torched side of Viribus B, he pealed his face off the pillow and reached out to the table next to his bed. His hand connected with a glass, knocking it to the floor.

"Damn."

Jagger opened a crusty eye and hoped to hell he'd remembered to take his DigiLenses out last night. The view of the room appeared unaugmented. Good.

The bed moaned as Jagger sat up on his elbows. He grabbed his uLink node off the bedside table and attached it to his neck. Using it, he think-told Ubiquity to patch him ClearHead. A faint whir came from the slim patch on his upper arm, and he felt a tiny prick on the skin. A moment later the drug flushed through his mind and his headache vanished. Next to him, the bed stirred and a woman's tight afro hair emerged from below the blanket. Neon fuchsia lines created an intricate pattern on her rich brown face, a tattoo style fashionable at the moment. Behind her, a blond man pulled back the blanket and sat up, his light skin unadorned, but around his neck he had the flaming eye pendent of the Lumen. *He's religious,* Jagger thought.

He'd never had time for anything like that. His parents worked as miners back when mining was still a viable option on Viribus B. Their workmanlike ethic hadn't left time for religion, old world or new. And as soon as he was old enough, Jagger joined the military to get away from the dreariness of home. For a while war had become his religion. His hip ached, forcing back memories of the battle of Ruyad. He patched NoPain and wished he could patch something to make him forget.

Jagger got out of bed, his feet cool in the pool of spilled water.

"Hey, time to go," he said to the sleepy figures in bed.

The girl rubbed a palm into her eye and yawned. "S'wrong Jason? I taut we brekchow?"

"Who's Jason?" Jagger said.

The woman frowned. "You, eh?"

"So I am," Jagger said. He picked up their clothes from the floor and threw it at them. "Now go."

The blond guy kissed his teeth. "Easy. We gone."

Jagger mopped up the water as the two got dressed and left his apartment. He stood, yawned, and stretched out his arms and back. He considered patching WideAwake, but instead think-told Ubiquity to make a pot of coffee for him. Then he headed for the shower to wash off the smell of last night.

#

The smell of coffee wafted over him when he stepped out of the shower. With the water shut off, he heard a delivery drone trying to access his drop-off box.

"Shit." He grabbed a towel and rushed back into the living area. The drop-off box stuck out of a window of his ninety-sixth-floor apartment. He'd told the managing agency it had been malfunctioning, but they'd done nothing about it. The drone, swaying wildly in the wind, tried to connect to his broken guide arm to dock. Jagger sighed and walked over to the drop-off box. He eased his upper body into the metal rectangle attached to his window and tried not to think of the long drop below him. He reached out, grabbed the docking arm and held it still for the drone. It attached to the drop-off box, and pulled itself closer. Jagger moved back to make room, just before the drone extended a section of itself into the metal rectangle.

The end of the drone lit up and began playing the logo of the delivery company.

"Greetings," a voice from the display said. "Would you like to pay the fee or see some specially selected adverts?"

"Give me the ads."

Immediately the display changed, and an advert played. The smell of the freshly made coffee filled Jagger's nostrils. He walked to his kitchen to get a cup. As soon as he turned, the advert stopped, and the voice spoke. "You must face the display within one meter for the advert to play."

Jagger sighed. "Okay, okay." He moved back to the display and watched five adverts for crap he'd never buy. Once happy, the drone deposited its load and detached itself from Jagger's drop-off box and spun away. Off to deliver more goods.

Jagger opened the box and looked at the jacket inside. The trip out by the hot edge to bring down the underage immersion gang had destroyed his last one. He threw the jacket on his bed, got himself a coffee and sat at his beaten up old table. He put his feet up on a nearby chair and think-told Ubiquity to show him a list of his current jobs. Two items appeared, floating in the air in front of him. One was a case he'd accepted, one was the request from Elkie. He ignored the request and opened the case he was working on. An image of Henry Jenkins replaced the list. Next to the image there were details of the case. His business partner thought Henry was stealing from him. He wanted Jagger to track Henry's meetings in immersion and report back on his activity.

Jagger looked at a list of immersions Henry had used recently. It was long. Jagger shook his head and closed the case file. He lacked motivation to look into Jenkins. Instead, he think-told Ubiquity to open the list Elkie had provided. The names of the N-Tac malfunction deaths appeared in front of him. Ubiquity asked if he'd like to mark the case as active? He told it to leave it as pending.

Jagger looked at the names. He took a sip of his coffee and told Ubiquity to give him the demographics on them. The list updated with extra details below each name. They were between eighteen and thirty, male, and from Viribus B or the Demesne system, with one Orinian. All were low income or unemployed, all except one. She appeared to be the daughter of a rich Orini financier, but she'd been on Viribus B when she'd died. Runaway from home, Jagger figured.

He asked Ubiquity to check the news reports for the names. A handful of reports came back of petty crimes, but none mentioned the N-Tac malfunctions. Next he asked Ubiquity to display the immersions people were using when the malfunctions happened. The new search came back blank. How could that be? Jagger took his feet off the chair and sat forward.

He asked Ubiquity why the lack of results. It informed him they had used a technology to mask their activity, mostly likely a VPN and proxy. It interested him they had all done that.

Jagger took a swig of his coffee. A couple of victims using a VPN he'd expect, but for every single person to have masked their activity seemed suspicious. Jagger decided to take a different tack. He stood and moved to the old immersion pod in the corner of his living area. Jagger picked up his well worn N-Tac and pulled the tight fitting plastimetal suit on. He paused, thinking about the malfunctions, and how he'd never considered that the suit he wore every day for work could kill him.

He shook his head and stepped into the immersion pod. Once inside, the pod gripped his suit and lifted him. It allowed him to move his arms and legs in any direction. When combined with the N-Tac suit and visuals through his DigiLenses, the sensation of being fully immersed was complete.

Jagger now floated in the center of a bubble made up of hundreds of video tiles with colors swirling behind them. Even after all this time, his home bubble still created a feeling of an awe within him. Immediately the view presented him with two options. Recorded or Live Immersions? He selected recorded and then YouImmerse, ignoring the other options. YouImmerse allowed ordinary people to upload immersive recordings of themselves. How good the sensation of immersion felt depended on the kit they could afford.

Jagger think-told Ubiquity to display recordings the victims had made in the last year. A huge list of video tiles appeared in the vast space in front of him. Jagger flicked through them, getting a short preview of them as he went. They were all the usual garbage young people uploaded. Either showing off with their friends or posting immersions of them doing whatever stupid dare was doing the rounds at the moment.

He sighed and cleared the list. Next he asked for recordings made by the parents or siblings of the victims. An even bigger list appeared. People loved showing off, didn't they? He cleared the list.

After a moment of floating in his bubble, it struck him. He asked Ubiquity to show recordings by the parents or siblings using the word malfunction. Three results appeared. Two from Deula City, on Tor Fosse in the Demesne system, and one from Pherson City, here on Viribus B.

Jagger selected the one from Pherson City to play. Everything flashed white, then he was stood in a tiny apartment in front of a woman frozen in time. Her name, Natalie Bevan, the immersion title and duration, floated in front of her. He gazed around him. Metal walls were rusted at the corners, and electrical wires hung from badly repaired units. The apartment was dark, apart from the pink and blue light coming in from a neon sign outside a window. And it was a mess. Clothes were scattered across the floor and chairs, the remains of several meals left to grow mold on a table. For once Jagger was glad smell wasn't one of the sensations captured by immersion.

He tried to move his body but found himself stuck in one position. Natalie didn't have a professional immersion recording setup. She had just used the recorder built into her home's Ubiquity terminal. Anyone interested in recording immersions usually had a setup of three recorders so you could move around the space. And the more money you spent, the better the experience became. Heat and wind sensors were common. Object mapping, so you'd hit objects rather than passing through them, was also standard for most amateur immersion creators. Some creators in Live Immersions even wore sensor suits, so you could feel and experience everything they did. But none came close to producing the experience you'd get in an immersion created by a professional studio. Music and film immersions were insane spectacles, and gaming took immersion to another level of intensity altogether.

Jagger brought his attention back to Natalie Bevan. She looked tired. Her short hair a mess, her tank top stained and off white. Jagger asked Ubiquity who she was related to on the list. The name Tsai Bevan appeared. He'd only died three weeks ago. Jagger acknowledged the information and told Ubiquity to play the immersion.

The scene at once came to life. Sound enveloped Jagger. At first it was jumble of noise. Then he picked out the sounds of people on a busy street below, talking and yelling. He heard the drone of rotocar engines, a lane must be somewhere near in the sky above. Within the room itself, a background hum of electricity permeated, and music from other resident's apartments leaked in. A flickering yellow bulb on Natalie's ceiling flushed out the pink and blue light that came in through the window.

"Fa cryin out loud," Natalie said. She reached up and smacked the light. It stopped flicking. Now animated, Jagger saw the tiredness on her face. The puffy red eyes. In her hand she held a crumpled tissue. Around her feet and on the table used tissues lay everywhere. She raised one to her nose and rubbed away snot that hung there. Her raw eyes stared directly into Jaggers.

"Sa, I... This no me usual thing, but I..." Natalie sighed and slumped to the sofa. "I don't na what ta do. Him gone. Me light Tsai is gone. I taught dis would help. To tell someone, ya know?" Natalie stared at the table in front of her, tears welled in her eyes. "A malfunction, dey say. A malfunction in dem blasted machine and mi poor boy is crush. Him look like a banana ya tro out. Skin black and bruised." Natalie sobbed. Jagger's instinct was to turn away from the scene, away from her pain, but the immersion wouldn't allow him.

"Dem come and give me what? Ten thousand credits." A hard look fell over Natalie's face.

"Ten thousand credits and we done. No investigation. Dis a normal ting they say. Malfunctions happen. They don't want ta know when I tell dem about da cult. They don't care. This a malfunction. Now mi don't care. Mi don't care."

Someone banging on the apartment door made Natalie jump. A muffled voice shouted something. Natalie stood. "Ya, me come."

The recording ended and booted Jagger back to the first frame. He sighed and exited back to his bubble. He'd hoped there'd be more. Tsai's mother was clearly upset, who wouldn't be losing their son like that. Jagger guessed she'd had a visit from Kolff-Ogogic. A nice few credits to keep her quiet. *Standard procedure for a corporate,* Jagger thought.

Then Natalie mentioned a cult, what had she meant? Jagger went back into the immersion and watched it again. There was nothing.

He stood in Natalie Bevan's frozen apartment and wondered what else there was to find. He scanned the room again. This time he paid more attention. The clothes scattered around the room were clearly a stripper's. On the table before Natalie, a small plastic bag stuck out from under a plate. Next to it a slate gray cylinder of a hypodermic lay used. Jagger looked at Natalie's arms. The faintest red dots along the area where veins were closest to the surface confirmed his suspicion.

Jagger swept the rest of the room with his eyes. The walls in the living area were bare except for the rust. Behind the sofa, a corridor led into darkness. Jagger think-told Ubiquity to increase the brightness. The details in the living area blew out in whiteness, but the dark corridor now revealed several doors. The two either side were closed, but the far one sat open. In the end room, sheets of paper were stuck to the wall. He couldn't make out the picture on the paper. He asked Ubiquity to zoom in and enhance the image. The image grew. Each piece of paper appeared to have a drawing on it. Jagger struggled to make out what the images were. One vaguely looked like a man, the other, a thick multi-colored line.

Jagger exited the recording and stepped out of his immersion pod. As he got dressed, he think-told Ubiquity to get Natalie Bevan's address and order him a SkyTaxi.

———

Dear reader,

If you enjoyed the sample of **Residuum Offerings: Voracious Universe Book One** you can buy it on pre-order now from Amazon.

Okay, until the next time, take it easy,
Ric Rae

<<<<>>>>

Printed in Great Britain
by Amazon